Bartlett

Bartlett

James T. Janson

Columbus, Ohio

This book is a work of fiction. The names, characters and events in this book are the products of the author's imagination or are used fictitiously. Any similarity to real persons living or dead is coincidental and not intended by the author.

The views and opinions expressed in this book are solely those of the author and do not reflect the views or opinions of Gatekeeper Press. Gatekeeper Press is not to be held responsible for and expressly disclaims responsibility of the content herein.

Bartlett

Published by Gatekeeper Press
2167 Stringtown Rd, Suite 109
Columbus, OH 43123-2989
www.GatekeeperPress.com

Copyright © 2021 by James T. Janson
All rights reserved. Neither this book, nor any parts within it may be sold or reproduced in any form or by any electronic or mechanical means, including information storage and retrieval systems, without permission in writing from the author. The only exception is by a reviewer, who may quote short excerpts in a review.

The interior formatting, typesetting, and editorial work for this book are entirely the product of the author. Gatekeeper Press did not participate in and is not responsible for any aspect of these elements.

Library of Congress Control Number: 2021936328

ISBN (paperback): 9781662912658

*This book is dedicated to my wife Eileen,
and my children
Jim, Matt, Kate, Meg, and Annie.
Without them I am nothing
With them I am everything*

Contents

Chapter 1: *Jimmy*   1

Chapter 2: *Elaine*   9

Chapter 3: *St. Rita School*   13

Chapter 4: *Terri*   17

Chapter 5: *Mildred*   21

Chapter 6: *Sister Mary Magdalene*   25

Chapter 7: *Drabek*   31

Chapter 8: *Tom Corbett*   37

Chapter 9: *Mr. Sheffield*   41

Chapter 10: *Field Trip*   45

Chapter 11: *Jimmy and Elaine*   51

Chapter 12: *Mildred and Elaine*   57

Chapter 13: *Mildred and Mae*   61

Chapter 14: *Strat-O-Flier*   65

Chapter 15: *Elaine and Mr. Sheffield*   69

Chapter 16: *The Astronaut*	71
Chapter 17: *Mr. Tagger*	75
Chapter 18: *Shepard*	79
Chapter 19: *Bartlett*	83
Chapter 20: *Confrontation*	89
Chapter 21: *And the winner is . . .*	91
Chapter 22: *Jimmy and Drabek*	97
Chapter 23: *Aftermath*	101
Chapter 24: *To the Rescue*	105
Chapter 25: *Countdown*	109
Chapter 26: *Letting Go*	117
Chapter 27: *Resolution*	121

SATTELITE FIRED BY SOVIETS: CIRCLING UNITED STATES 15 TIMES A DAY
---Cleveland Plain Dealer announces launch of Sputnik, October 5, 1957

"Well, space is there and we're going to climb it, and the moon and planets are there, and new hopes for knowledge and peace are there. And, therefore, as we set sail, we ask God's blessing on the most hazardous and dangerous and greatest adventure on which man has ever embarked."
----John F. Kennedy, Moon Speech, Rice University, May 25, 1961

Chapter 1

Jimmy

Twelve-year-old Jimmy Dixon pedaled his red J.C. Higgins bicycle as fast as he could to 'the corner.' He had just earned a dime from his father for cutting the lawn. Multi-colored plastic streamers fluttered from the grips of his handlebars like gas jets. Red, green, yellow, blue! The humid August air caused beads of sweat to roll across his forehead. Jimmy took the shortcut to 'the corner,' a narrow dirt bike path that cut a diagonal swath across a small, open field. Along the left edge of the bumpy path as it veered slightly to the right grew a thick hedge of wild blackberry bushes. Most days, Jimmy would hit the brakes of his bike and stop to pick a handful of the sweet fruit. But today was different.

For Jimmy and his friends, 'the corner' was code for the Rexall Pharmacy. Rexall sat at the crossroads of Aurora Road and SOM Center, the main intersection in town. SOM stood for Solon, Orange, and Mayfield, the three communities through which the road ran. Solon, Ohio was Jimmy's town. Rexall Pharmacy was housed in the Solon Center Building occupying the southwest corner of Aurora Road and SOM. Sargent's grocery store, the Solon Post Office, and Donald Langley's office were also tenants of the building. Dr. Langley, the local dentist, was on the top floor. Across the street, two corners were occupied by gas stations, Standard Oil and Sunoco. On the fourth corner sat Roger's Bar, next to which was Pete's Barber Shop, next to which was Les' Open Kitchen.

As Jimmy approached Rexall Pharmacy, he leaned to the left, slammed on the brakes of his J.C. Higgins, and fishtailed to a stop. Two other bikes stood just outside the entrance of the pharmacy like horses at a hitching post. Jimmy flipped down the kickstand and hurried into Rexall. To his right was a double-tiered magazine stand, stocked with the latest film, fashion, music and adventure stories: *Argosy, Mademoiselle, Life, Look, True Confessions, Hit Parader, Silver Screen, Mad.* Jimmy's usual ritual was to sneak a peek at the cover of the current *Man's Action* magazine promising an illustrated eyeful of beautiful females, always seconds away from being torn apart by stiletto-clawed tigers or exploited by women-hungry pirates. Yet today was different. Even the August issue, boldly declaring "I Saw the Fertility Orgy of the Nhanga Pygmies," could not tempt him to plunge into the bowels of the magazine.

He glanced briefly toward the back of the drugstore

where Mr. Knapp, the pharmacist, clacked away on his mist green Remington Quiet-Riter typewriter, busily creating prescription labels. Mr. Knapp paid no attention to Jimmy who spotted his friend, Doll, sitting at the marble-top counter of the soda fountain crunching on a pretzel rod and sipping his second cherry Coke of the morning. One year younger than Jimmy, Bobby Shiver and his family lived next door to the Dixons. Bobby's Grandma Reich always called him her 'Dolly Boy' which he hated, but Doll suited him just fine. Seated next to Doll was Lee Kolls, a classmate of Jimmy's at St. Rita School in Solon.

"Hey, Jimmy," Lee said, "you sleep in today?"

"I had to cut the grass early, Mom's having her ladies bridge club over this afternoon. She wants everything to look perfect inside and out."

Marge Dixon's 'ladies bridge club' was composed of mothers from 'the five families.' The Dixon, Shiver, and Swanson families lived on Linden Drive, which was Jimmy's street. The Soederbergs and Ryans lived on Baldwin Road, one street over.

"Well, are they here?" Jimmy asked excitedly.

With a wink of his eye and a knowing smile, Lee spun Jimmy's red, padded chrome stool a half turn perfectly timed to stop and direct his pal's gaze at the sweet treasures in front of them across the aisle. Just this morning Mr. Knapp had resupplied the candy display with fresh boxes of Chuckles,

Tootsie Rolls, Necco Wafers, Chunky, Bit-O-Honey, Sky Bars, and other tempting treats that Jimmy and his friends loved to spend their lawn cutting or snow shoveling money on.

But Jimmy was on a mission. He scanned the candy display top to bottom, side to side. Suddenly, there it was: an unopened red and yellow rectangular box of Topps baseball cards. Jimmy leaped from his stool, nearly bowling over Mr. Knapp who had stepped away from his prescription labels to personally open the box of Topps cards.

"Here you are Jimmy, hot off the shelf," said Mr. Knapp, who knew how dedicated the boy was to his card collection. The pharmacist carefully removed the top of the box and offered Jimmy first choice. The wax packs of cards were yellow with the word "baseball" in blue lettering set inside a baseball pictured on the front. Above the baseball, was the word "Topps," and below the baseball, in red lettering were the words "Bubble Gum 5c."

The buzz around the neighborhood was that the final set of Topps cards would soon be available in late August. Here they were right before Jimmy's eyes. By the end of July, he had collected most of the cards needed at that point to complete the entire series by summer's end. Yet, one card continued to elude him, Early Wynn card #1. Wynn originally pitched for the Cleveland Indians,

Jimmy's team, but was traded to the Chicago White Sox after the 1957 season. For some unknown reason Wynn's card was scarce, possibly because it was the first numbered in the entire 1960 set. No one in Jimmy's neighborhood had it. Jimmy *had* to have it.

So did Dennis Drabek, another of his classmates, who would go to any length to beat Jimmy in obtaining the elusive card #1. Including cheating. When Mr. Knapp was occupied with his prescription labels, Drabek would innocently sneak over to the candy display, carefully unseal a Topps wax pack, and shuffle through the cards. If a new player were inside, he would purchase the pack. If not, he would rewrap the cards, sliding them underneath the remaining packs in the Topps box. He even had the nerve to boldly accuse *Jimmy* of opening Topps packs illegally to look for players to add to his collection. His hope was that Mr. Knapp would bar Jimmy from entering Rexall Pharmacy. But the pharmacist would not buy it. Dennis's notoriety as a troublemaker was all too familiar around the neighborhood.

As Jimmy was about to hand the pharmacist his dime for two fresh Topps packs, Mr. Knapp interrupted. "Just to let you know, Jimmy, there were a few packs remaining in the old box which I replaced with this new one. I set them in that round wicker basket at the end of the soda fountain counter. Perhaps you would like to choose from those cards?"

Jimmy remained firm. There was no way in the world that

Early Wynn would be in that wicker basket. If no one had gotten him by now, with the baseball season winding down, then he had to be included somewhere in the last series of cards.

"Thanks anyhow, Mr. Knapp, but I'll go with the new packs. Here's my dime."

Jimmy turned and sprinted out the door of Rexall Pharmacy with Doll racing close behind. He wanted to savor the opening of these two new Topps packs in the warm late summer sunshine. Opening the first pack he reached for the hard rectangle of pink bubble gum contained within and plopped it into his mouth.

"Frank Malzone, got 'em!" "Jimmy Piersall, got 'em!" "Willie Tasby, got 'em!" "YEEESS! Harry Chiti, don't have!" Jimmy pulled the final two cards from the pack. "Got 'em both," he shrugged. "OK, I guess, one new player. It's a start."

Just as Jimmy was about to tear open the second wax pack, Lee came charging out of Rexall screaming, "I GOT HIIIIIIM!!! EARLY WYYYYYN!!!" Jimmy was stunned. "Early Wynn, no way! I knew it, he just had to be somewhere in the last series of new cards."

"But that's not where I got him," Lee responded. "The basket at the end of the soda fountain counter, you know, the one Mr. Knapp mentioned to you, that's where he was! Three packs were there, I had a nickel left to spend so, I reached in and paid Mr. Knapp. How lucky is that?"

"Yeah, lucky," groaned Jimmy. He was happy for Lee, but he sure wanted Early Wynn. He was so close, a baseball bat length away from that round wicker basket.

"Don't worry, Jimmy," joked Lee. "I'll remember to leave you Early Wynn in my will someday!"

"Thanks, pal," shouted Jimmy as the three boys sped away on their bikes towards the dirt path and the wild blackberry bushes. Summer break was almost over. There was not a minute to lose. His second unopened wax pack was all but forgotten.

Chapter 2

Elaine

"Elaine, Elaine, open this door immediately!"

Elaine Shiver rolled her eyes in frustration. "I'll call you back later, Sue," she said. "Mom's on the warpath."

Hopping off her bed, the fourteen-year-old ran to open the door. "How many times have I forbidden you to lock yourself in your room?" shouted her mother, Mildred.

"But Mom, a woman needs her privacy," pleaded Elaine.

"Not in my house," her mother countered. "And you are not a woman, you're a girl! Now get downstairs this minute, there's dishes, dusting and vacuuming to be done."

"And turn off that ridiculous music!"

Teen Angel faded from Mildred's ears as she stomped down the hall and down the steps into the living room. Elaine was not unlike most teenage girls her age. Almost! Sure, she read *Hit Parader* magazine, listened to Elvis, Frankie, and Little Richard, watched *Leave it to Beaver* and loved talking to boys. Yet, Elaine was determined not to be like her mother or any of the women in Mildred's bridge club, always expected to have home-cooked meals ready for the family at 5pm. Let alone tending, cooking, sewing, cleaning, laundry, and grocery shopping. She was supposed to keep the home fires burning while the man of the family, Elaine's father Ed, brought home the paycheck. Although she loved her father dearly, he made it clear to her mother who was king of the castle. Given an "allowance" for food, clothing, and cleaning supplies, Mildred had no say in money matters.

Elaine loved adventure. When Davy Crockett was all the rage, she asked her dad to buy her a coonskin cap. She even collected Davy Crockett trading cards. Her favorite comic strips were *Steve Canyon* and *Dick Tracy*. Stories she read of Robert Peary's race to the North Pole or Thor Heyerdahl's Kon-Tiki expedition across the Pacific tantalized her imagination. Yet, something was radically wrong in Elaine's mind: Davy, Steve, Dick, Robert, Thor. "Why always the men?" she questioned. Michelangelo, Newton, Columbus, all hailed for their achievements, all great *men*? In her world of stay home wives, and the occasional working woman relegated to the role of secretary, what did one expect? The achievements of Charles Lindbergh always prefaced any discussion of the exploits of Amelia Earhart; Madame Curie by Albert Einstein; Pocahontas by John Rolfe.

The launching of Sputnik by the Soviet Union in 1957 changed Elaine's life forever. Her dream focused on becoming an astronomer, exploring the planets and stars, even traveling in space someday. She imagined climbing aboard a rocket ship heading to the moon or Mars. For Christmas she asked for a telescope rather than clothes, shoes, or a cuddly teddy bear. She did not want to look back someday at what might have been, what she may have been able to do with whatever talents she possessed if only she had gotten an education instead of getting married at an early age. Even if it was accepted as right for a woman in 1960.

"I will not be my mother," vowed Elaine as she turned off her record player and closed the bedroom door behind her with authority.

Chapter 3

St. Rita School

Labor Day came way too quickly for Jimmy. It meant that summer was at an end and school would begin. His days of playing pick-up baseball games, riding around Solon on his bike with his pals, playing cowboys and Indians, reading the adventures of the Hardy Boys on rainy days, and staying out until dark playing tag with kids in the neighborhood were now over.

This year Jimmy would be in seventh grade at St. Rita School. His mother, Marge, had attended a parent-teacher's meeting last week and was told that Sister Mary Magdalene, a member of the Vincentian Sisters of Charity serving the parish of St. Rita Church, would be his teacher this year. Sister Magdalene was reported to be a nice person but very plain looking. Certainly not like Sister Mary David, Jimmy's sixth-grade teacher. Sister David was young and beautiful. Why did she decide to become a nun? thought Jimmy and his school buddies. She was too good looking. Only God knew!

Jimmy liked school. His favorite subjects were history and art although when asked which he preferred best he would always say neither. I love recess, was his reply. A lame joke even for a twelve-year-old. To be truthful, history was first and foremost in Jimmy's world. Stories of the explorations of Vasco da Gama, Ferdinand Magellan and Henry Hudson appealed to his imagination and sense of adventure. But it was Christopher Columbus who Jimmy always chose to be when he and his friends played explorer in the fields and woods surrounding the frog pond near his home. "I have come to proclaim this land for Spain," Jimmy exclaimed as he lifted a foot upon a large boulder which lay a few yards away from the pond. In fact, the boulder was a multi-purpose prop for Jimmy and his friends. Other days, it would protect them from Indian attacks, arrows whistling precariously overhead. Other times, as a meteor from space the large stone was forbidding and mysterious.

The one subject Jimmy absolutely hated was math. He simply could not grasp the concept of numbers. Addition and subtraction were fine (although he always needed to count on his fingers), but when it came to fractions or equations and everything in between he was terrified. When the teacher would randomly call upon students to answer a math question Jimmy would gaze down at the top of his desk pretending to be concentrating on working out the problem. "Please, God, …please, God, not me this time," he prayed.

But the outright worst were the story problems. The death knell for Jimmy were the words "show your work." Sure, he could guess the answer, but what were the odds; a trillion to one? There was no way! Jimmy slowly lifted his head, only to lock eyes with his teacher. "Jimmy, please come to the board to work out the next story problem. And be sure to show your work!"

Chapter 4

Terri

"Speed it up, Jimmy, or we'll be late for practice," shouted Lee. It was mid-November and the snow had arrived early in northeastern Ohio. Shortcutting through neighborhood backyards, the two boys crossed over the railroad tracks, skirting Aurora Road shopping center as they trekked their way towards Solon Road School gym. As the wind and snow increased, Jimmy barely noticed. Although it was Friday and basketball practice would only run two hours tonight rather than the usual three, his mind was a million miles away.

For Jimmy, baseball was king. In fact, at summers' end, his Little League teammates had voted him their most valuable player. He did it all for the Tigers on the baseball diamond. Whether stretched out horizontally to backhand a scorching line drive at shortstop or roping a double up the gap in left centerfield, Jimmy was a whiz. Basketball was a different matter. He could not shoot, his dribbling was lame, and his defense was pathetic. Jimmy's coordination on the diamond fell flat as a deflated balloon on the hardcourt. Yet, he loved being on the St. Rita seventh-grade basketball team. It did not bother him at all to be riding the bench with limited playing time. Being with his school pals, joking and having fun, counted most for Jimmy. Plus, his coach, Mr. Lloyd, was a nice man.

But it was Terri Lloyd, the coach's daughter, who caught Jimmy's eye the very first day she walked into his fifth-grade class as a transfer student from Florida. Up to that time, girls were rarely on his radar. Sure, Cecilia Heffernen was his first puppy love back in the second grade. Yet when Cecilia began to 'like' Walter Weber that was that. No more girls for Jimmy, just baseball and Christopher Columbus. Until Terri arrived.

Terri was as cute as a button with her black pixie-cut hairstyle framing her gently freckled cheeks and a winning smile. But it was Terri's personality which set her apart from the other girls in his class. She was smart and fun loving, but above all, kind and caring. Jimmy was in love with her from the beginning. Well, as in love as a twelve-year old boy could be. To add icing to Jimmy's grade school cake, Terri was also a cheerleader for the seventh-grade boys basketball team. So were Doreen Downy, Diane Hoff, Janie Englebrecht, and Andrea Schmader. Sitting on the bench most of the time did have its benefits, allowing him to watch cheerleading routines.

During tonight's basketball practice Mr. Lloyd would

again see Jimmy shoot his usual complement of air balls, allow opposing players to steal the ball from him, and continue to defend like a girl, but so what! As he and Lee walked into Solon Road School gym with only minutes to spare Jimmy was dreaming of what was to take place *after* practice. It was the fourth Friday of the month, which meant the school skating party at nearby Geauga Lake Park roller rink. It also meant that Terri would be there.

The monthly skating party was sponsored and chaperoned by the St. Rita Parent's Club. Geauga Lake was an amusement park just beyond the Solon city limits in the township of Aurora. Although closed for the season, the park was the setting for the St. Rita end-of-the-school-year picnic in late May. Thrill rides such as the Wild Mouse, Dutch Shoes, and Tilt-a-Whirl scared Jimmy to death. But it was The Clipper, a wooden roller coaster, with a first hill height of 65 feet which left him completely terrified. He avoided the beast at all costs. The only exception was the school picnic, when he put on his best face, white knuckling through every numbing twist and turn The Clipper had to offer. Especially with Terri, cool and calm, sitting at his side.

Jimmy was only slightly more coordinated with roller skates tied to his feet than he was with a basketball in his hand. Inching his way to the edge of the rink, he felt like a penguin on ice. Once he got his bearings, however, the whir of rolling wheels and rhythm of the Hammond Organ playing a jaunty tune boosted his confidence. As always, there would be the occasional butt slam to the wooden floor accompanied by hearty laughter from his buddies. Slamming his knee into the low iron fence exiting the rink toward the refreshment center was especially painful. *When on Earth will I learn how to stop properly?* Jimmy wondered.

But it was worth it. Jimmy's pride would be resurrected with the final skate of the evening . . . The Grand March! Couples lining up single file holding hands or arms gently curved around a partner's waist would romantically traverse the perimeter of the rink to a beautiful organ rendition of *Theme from a Summer Place*. It was the closest Jimmy could get to Terri without being warned by the nuns to "leave room for the Holy Ghost" while slow dancing at a St. Rita School dance.

"Jimmy, let's go!" Lee shouted. "Mr. Haas is waiting to drive us to Geauga Lake."

"Be right there." With basketball in hand, he took one final shot. "Swish!" Nothing but net! "Looks like I'm in for a good night," Jimmy thought. He grabbed his jacket and ran out the gym door.

Chapter 5

Mildred

"Elaine, please hurry, will you? The ladies will be here in five minutes. You need to leave for work immediately." Mildred Shiver hesitated a moment, surveying the neatly appointed card table awaiting the arrival of her monthly women's bridge club.

"Coming right down, Mom! "

As Elaine flew out the front door, she sprinted past Millie Soederberg and Mae Ryan who were walking up the driveway. Marge Dixon and Evelyn Swanson would not be far behind. "Have fun today ladies, hope you win at cards," yelled Elaine as she hopped on her aqua colored, Roadmaster Jet Pilot bicycle and sped off through the snow to her part-time weekend job working the soda fountain at Rexall Pharmacy.

Mildred was relieved to see Elaine leave the house. She simply did not want her around when the bridge ladies arrived. She was embarrassingly different, quite unlike the daughters of Mae, Marge, and Evelyn. Millie Soederberg had three sons, yet she understood the rebel in Elaine as did the others.

An hour earlier, Mildred and Elaine had been locked in a shouting match. "I just cannot believe you sometimes, Elaine, I mean what are you thinking half the time?" demanded Mildred. "Robert Friedrich asked you to the winter ball at school and you refused? Why, Elaine, why?"

"But Mom, I don't want to go to the dance and certainly not with Robert Friedrich. He's a creep. Besides, I have other things to do with my time," countered Elaine.

"Can't you understand, Robert comes from a very important Solon family. His father is president of National Trust Bank. Mrs. Friedrich stands to inherit a fortune when her mother Gertrude dies."

Elaine's voice rose two octaves, "I could care less!" she shouted back.

"Think of your future, Elaine. You need to be popular. Do you understand? Popular! When the right boy comes along, like Robert Friedrich, you will fall in love and be the proper wife."

"That may be fine for you Mom, but I have my eye on something greater than Robert Friedrich . . . outer space!"

"Oh please, Elaine, not that fantasy again," Mildred's frustration growing. "Space is for men. Your place is here on Earth with your husband and children."

"You just don't get it do you, Mom?" shouted Elaine as she ran upstairs to her bedroom. "Robert Friedrich is still a creep!"

As Mildred stalked into the kitchen, her frustration with Elaine was soon forgotten. She had to prepare for the bridge club. "Everything must be perfect," she thought aloud. Cucumber tea sandwiches – thin and trimmed of crust. Apple salad with cherry Jell-O. Cream scones to accompany a cup of coffee. "The ladies will be so impressed."

Chapter 6

Sister Mary Magdalene

Two days before Christmas vacation, Jimmy's class was introduced by Sister Mary Magdalene to the Mercury astronauts. Three years earlier, the space race began with the 1957 launch of the Soviet satellite Sputnik 1. This came as a shock to the American public and led to the creation of NASA. After the successful launch of the Explorer 1 satellite in 1958, manned spaceflight became the next goal for the United States. Thus, the Mercury Seven was born, and the group of seven Mercury astronauts were announced by NASA on April 9, 1959. They would pilot the manned spaceflights of the Mercury program.

Jimmy had not given much thought to exploring outer space. Sure, Sister Magdalene had taught them about the nine planets of the Solar System in the Milky Way galaxy. She even recruited the school maintenance man, Mr. Bender, to suspend from the classroom ceiling her handmade model of the planets orbiting around the sun. The mobile consisted of Styrofoam balls of varied sizes, spray-painted different colors to represent each planet . . . blue for Venus, red for Mars, green for Earth and so on. Pluto, the smallest planet, was yellow.

But Jimmy never actually considered anyone *traveling* to those far off worlds. Certainly not Columbus or Balboa or Magellan or even himself for that matter. But Sister Mary Magdalene changed everything. The Mercury astronauts were his new heroes.

"Now class, I have an early Christmas gift for all of you," declared Sister Magdalene. The smiling nun carefully tore open a large manila envelope. "A few weeks ago," she said proudly, "I took it upon myself to write NASA, requesting a group photograph be sent to me of the Mercury Seven. In fact, one picture for each of you."

Sister Magdalene walked down each aisle of the classroom stopping to personally hand every student a photograph of the seven astronauts.

"Merry Christmas, Joseph," she smiled.

"Merry Christmas, Lee."

"Merry Christmas, Terri."

"Merry Christmas, Victor."

Jimmy could hardly contain himself as Sister Magdalene drew closer to his desk.

"Merry Christmas, Doreen."

"Merry Christmas, Eileen."

Sister Magdalene paused before Jimmy's desk, then

gently handed him a photograph. Seven astronauts, standing elbow to elbow and dressed in full space suits, stared back at him from the glossy black and white image. Each was identified by reproduced signatures scrawled above their heads. M. Scott Carpenter, Leroy G. Cooper, Jr., John H. Glenn, Jr., Virgil I. Grissom, Walter M. Schirra, Jr., Alan B. Shepard Jr., Donald K. Slayton. Jimmy was mesmerized.

"Merry Christmas, Jimmy."

"Merry Christmas, Jimmy."

"Merry Chris . . ." Suddenly Jimmy's head snapped back.

"Oh, uh! Sorry Sister Mary Magdalene, I didn't mean to be rude. It's just that I . . ."

"No need to apologize," smiled the nun. "I understand."

"Merry Christmas to you too, Sister. And thank you for teaching us about the Mercury astronauts."

Sister Mary Magdalene stood before the class. "Now that you have received your photographs, I want you to sit quietly at your desks to await the arrival of our pastor, Monsignor Mazer, who has a special announcement to share with you all."

Soon there was a gentle knock on the classroom door. John Marshall, the official door monitor, jumped from his seat. "Good morning," he cheerfully said, as the portly Monsignor Mazer walked into the classroom.

"Class," Sister Magdalene reminded as if on cue.

"Good morning, Monsignor Mazer," the students

responded in unison!

"Thank you, students," said the Monsignor. "With only a few days before the start of your Christmas vacation, Sister Mary Magdalene asked me to visit with you briefly this morning to announce an exciting opportunity for your class. With such interest in space exploration these days, NASA has announced a five-city traveling exhibition co-sponsored with the Smithsonian Institution in Washington, D. C. regarding Project Mercury and the seven Mercury astronauts. The first stop on the tour will be our very own Public Hall in downtown Cleveland. The exhibition will open a week after the New Year. With that in mind, I have enthusiastically given Sister Magdalene permission to arrange a field trip for your class to Public Hall in mid-February. That should give Sister a few more weeks after your Christmas vacation to further explore the mission of NASA with you and the dream of someday landing on the moon or beyond. In addition, Sister will soon be announcing to you a class essay contest based on the American space program. The winner will receive a very nice prize."

Jimmy was more than excited. "How cool is that? A field trip to Public Hall," he whispered to Lee across the aisle. "Yeah, neat," his pal replied.

"A free day from school," muttered Dennis Drabek, the class bully, from the back of the room.

"What a loser," thought Jimmy."

"Well, Sister Magdalene, I must visit other classrooms before the end of the school day. Thank you for giving me the opportunity to speak with your students."

"You are very welcome, Monsignor."

"Now class," Sister announced, "who would like to ask Monsignor for his blessing?" A forest of hands immediately shot towards Heaven, many shaking vigorously to gain Sister Magdalene's visual attention.

"Beth Dalton, you may have the honor," proclaimed the nun.

"Monsignor," Beth asked reverently, "may we please have your blessing?"

With that, the students arose from their seats and proceeded to kneel next to their desks, hands folded perfectly with bodies ramrod straight.

"May Almighty God bless you in the name of the Father and of the Son and of the Holy Ghost, Amen."

"Merry Christmas, students!" shouted Monsignor Mazer joyfully as he walked towards the classroom door. "And a very Happy New Year!"

A few seconds later, the school bell rang. Perfect timing.

"You may have your lunch now students," declared Sister Magdalene as a mother would to her children. "If you plan to go outside for recess, be sure to bundle up warm. It's very snowy and cold today."

Chapter 7

Drabek

Jimmy gobbled down his lunch. With half a sandwich in his hand, he slipped on his heavy winter coat, pulled his brown leather cap over his head, flaps down, buckled his black rubber boots, and fast-walked down the hallway and out the main entrance of St. Rita School. He raced towards Lee and his pals, charging a group of sixth-grade boys standing atop a large mound of snow at the playground's edge, compliments of the school janitor Mr. Bender and his snowplow. They were determined to claim the mound for the seventh-grade class.

"Yessss, King of the Mountain!" shouted Jimmy enthusiastically. As he continued running to join the attack, he was struck in the back of the head by a large snowball. It nearly sent him sprawling to the ground. Regaining his momentum, he spun around angrily only to be pelted in the chest by three more snowy missiles. Before him stood Dennis Drabek, flanked by his two toadies Victor Praser and Frank Shorts.

Absolutely no one at St. Rita School, other than his toadies, liked Dennis Drabek. Pudgy in build and sloppy in appearance, he delighted in frightening students with his size and menacing glare. Each time Carolyn Menard, the most timid and shy girl in Jimmy's class, walked past him in the hall, Drabek would quickly flatten himself against the wall to avoid contact with her while yelling "Menard bugs! Menard bugs!" at the top of his voice. When raisins were discovered at the bottom of Sister Mary Magdalene's classroom aquarium, causing every fish to be found floating lifeless along the top of the water, all fingers pointed to Drabek. "Why look at me?" he pleaded, throwing up his arms. "I don't even like raisins!"

Drabek's reputation as a mischief-maker at St. Rita School began as early as the first grade. One time, during morning prayer, his teacher, Sister Mary Helen, caught Dennis pulling the pigtails of Susan Truby who sat in silence at her desk in front of him. Small but mighty, the feisty nun stormed down the aisle, grabbed Drabek by his shirt collar and escorted him into the hallway. The students cheered gleefully as the classroom door slammed shut behind them.

"I've just about had it with your antics, Mr. Drabek," said an exasperated Sister Helen. "You are to march immediately to the principles' office and explain to Sister Mary Celeste why you were sent by me. Sister will determine your punishment as she sees fit. NOW GO!"

Sister Mary Celeste sat working busily at her desk. Suddenly, Dennis Drabek stood before her, an angelic smile on his face. "Shouldn't you be in class now, Mr. Drabek?" she questioned.

"Good morning, Sister Mary Celeste," Dennis said sweetly. "Sister Mary Helen sent me to your office to brighten your day with a song. We had a singing contest in our class, and I was the winner."

"How sweet of Sister to think of me," the principle said gratefully. Then clearing a spot on her desk, she gently picked up the first grader and stood him on top of it. "My desk is your stage," Sister Mary Celeste declared. "You may begin now, please."

Continuing to smile pleasantly, Dennis began:

"*I'm a little teapot*

Short and stout.

Here is my handle,

Here is my spout.

When I get all steamed up

Hear me shout:

Tip me over

And pour me out!"

His song completed; Dennis bowed respectfully to Sister Mary Celeste.

"Well done, Mr. Drabek," said the principle, clapping

enthusiastically. "You may now return to your classroom. Your wonderful song certainly made my day!"

That evening while the nuns of St. Rita sat enjoying their evening meal in the dining room of their convent, Sister Mary Celeste leaned across the table to address Sister Mary Helen. "What a pleasant surprise it was for you to send Dennis Drabek to my office to sing *I'm a Little Teapot*. He has quite a nice singing voice."

Early the following morning, Dennis Drabek once again stood in Sister Mary Celeste's office. Standing next to him was Sister Mary Helen.

Drabek seemed to take special delight in going out of his way to ridicule Jimmy. Why exactly, Jimmy did not know. Yet, it may have started two summers ago when he drilled a two out Drabek fastball down the right field line driving in the winning runs in the Solon Little League championship game. The burly lefthander slammed his glove to the ground in frustration and cried all the way to the bench amid a roar of laughter from Jimmy and his teammates.

But it was Terri's obvious affection for Jimmy that really made him furious. "She's my girl," he would fantasize. Despite all his efforts to play the cool cat and man of the world to impress her, Terri turned the other way. "There is no way in the world that I will ever be your partner in The Grand March," she emphatically told him at a Geauga Lake school skating party. "Come on Jimmy, take my hand, let's skate together."

Drabek was seething. "You'll regret this, Terri. You and your weasel of a friend."

"Drop dead, Drabek!" Terri answered fearlessly.

With that, the school bully snapped. He charged Terri and Jimmy. But his skate caught on a dried piece of bubble gum stuck to the rink floor causing his roller to lock abruptly. In an instant his legs shot out and up in front of him resulting in a loss of momentum and a resounding thud as his body came crashing to the ground, rear end first. A crowd of skaters, who by that time had come over to witness the confrontation between Drabek and Terri, erupted with delight.

"Drop dead, Drabek!"

"Drop dead, Drabek!"

"Drop dead, Drabek!"

The chant reverberated throughout the rink. The bully, with Praser and Shorts in tow, half skated, half crawled to the edge of the rink, quickly unlaced his skates, and ran out the door.

Jimmy brushed the snow from the front of his winter coat and glared at Drabek. "Wow, real brave, Dennis," he mocked. "You need Praser and Shorts to protect you because you can't take me on your own."

"Now hear this, Dixon," Drabek countered. "You know

that essay contest Magdalene announced today? The one about space and the astronauts and all that boring stuff I can care less about. Well, I overheard you tell Kolls how much you wanted to win it. But you never will," he sneered. "I'm going to do everything I can to make sure you don't. Then Terri will not like you anymore. Hey, she may even start to like me, right?"

Chapter 8

Tom Corbett

Christmas was only three days away when the doorbell rang at the Dixon home. Jimmy bounded down the stairs from his bedroom two steps at a time. He opened the front door and then froze, not comprehending what he saw. Terri Lloyd stood in the doorway.

"Hi, Jimmy," said Terri cheerfully, "I hope I'm not disturbing you or your family."

Jimmy gathered himself from his initial shock. "Hi Terri," was all he could reply for a moment. Finally, "What are you doing here?"

"Dad's waiting in the car, so I only have a few minutes, besides, it is pretty cold standing here."

"Oh sure, sorry, Terri. Come on in," said Jimmy, embarrassed. Jimmy poked his head out the door giving a quick wave to his coach Mr. Lloyd.

As Terri took two steps into the foyer, she reached into a Higbee's Department Store shopping bag pulling out a small package neatly wrapped in colorful Christmas paper, perfectly tied up with a red ribbon bow.

"Merry Christmas," said Terri as she handed the package to a very surprised Jimmy. "Go ahead, open it. Christmas is still a few days away, but I won't tell anyone. Promise!"

Excited, Jimmy carefully opened the mystery package. Once unwrapped, he held a book in his hand, *Stand by for Mars*. Staring back at him from the cover of the dust jacket was a young man standing on a cratered, moon-like surface, his head enveloped in a clear space helmet. In the background was a rocket flying among the stars and the planet Saturn looming just above the horizon.

"Terri, I'm confused," said Jimmy, "our class already had its gift exchange a few weeks ago. Danny Hladnik gave me a box of pencils with my name printed on each of them."

"I know," replied Terri. "I got a Rudolph the Reindeer Christmas ornament from Cathy Craemer."

"So why this book?"

"Well, I saw how interested you were in learning about the Mercury astronauts from Sister Mary Magdalene and when Monsignor Mazer announced our class trip to Public Hall and the essay contest you nearly jumped out of your desk. So, I thought you would like this book as a special Christmas gift from me. It's a Tom Corbett, Space Cadet story."

"But Terri, I don't have a gift for you," lamented Jimmy.

"It's okay, Jimmy. As I said, this is something special. I better go now before Dad begins beeping the horn." Terri quickly took a step towards Jimmy and gently kissed him on the cheek. Then she was gone.

That night Jimmy dreamed twice. The first dream was Christmas morning when Santa brought him two more books in the Tom Corbett, Space Cadet series. The second dream was Terri kissing him on his other cheek.

Chapter 9

Mr. Sheffield

Elaine sat reading at her desk awaiting the arrival of her ninth-grade history teacher. Moments later, Mr. Sheffield entered the classroom and instantly turned toward the second row of students.

"February 22, 1732."

"David?"

David Parks looked up timidly from his desk. "Washington's birthday?"

"Are you asking me or telling me?" countered Mr. Sheffield.

David's brow tensed as he quietly prayed for what he hoped would be the correct answer. "Telling?"

"Correct! July 4, 1776."

Elaine quickly raised her hand but was ignored by Mr. Sheffield who nodded toward Kevin Porter seated two desks behind her.

"Uhh, I don't know," was the student's embarrassed response.

A second attempt to gain her teacher's attention ended in frustration for Elaine. Miffed by the obvious lack of interest from the boys, Mr. Sheffield decided to inform the class himself. "The signing of the Declaration of Independence!" Then he paused for a moment, emphatically tapping the large globe which sat upon his desk. "Christmas vacation has been over for two weeks now. You *men* should know these events if you want to amount to anything in life!"

"October 4, 1957."

Silence.

"Gentlemen?"

An unenthusiastic chorus of voices arose from Elaine's male classmates. "Sputnik launched."

"Ahh, so you *are* listening," replied Mr. Sheffield with a tinge of sarcasm.

He retrieved a pile of papers from his desk and proceeded to personally return them to each student. "For the most part, class, your essays titled *What Will the Future Bring?* were generally well written, although some not so. Grades with comments are indicated on each cover page. Also, a reminder that your second essay *My American Hero* is due next Wednesday. And ladies, that does not mean Mr. Elvis Presley."

"Excellent work Mr. Marsh, as always."

"Nicely written as well, Mr. Haas."

"You need to review your grammar, Miss Lucey."

"Very insightful, Mr. Flanders."

Unceremoniously and without comment Mr. Sheffield dropped Elaine's essay on her desk and walked on. A large grade of D jumped from the cover page. It was circled for emphasis. TOO BROAD! UNREALISTIC! DIDN'T WANT A PAPER BASED ON FICTION!!

"Students, if you need to discuss with me comments I have written on your essays I will be glad to do so after class. Now let us continue our study of the American Civil War as our country celebrates the centennial anniversary of that tragic conflict. As promised, Mr. Joseph Thompson will tell us the story of how his great, great, great grandmother invited to dinner both President Lincoln *and* General Grant at the same time." Joseph talked to the class for about fifteen minutes.

Elaine did not hear one word of what he said. Staring into space, she could only shake her head in frustration.

Chapter 10

Field Trip

"Today is going to be so cool," shouted Jimmy as he hopped into the seat next to his pal Lee. It was mid-week, and his class was about to embark on a forty-minute drive to downtown Cleveland to see the exhibition about Project Mercury.

"Now class," said Sister Mary Magdalene, "Before our bus driver, Mr. Kinderly, leaves the school yard let us pray together to St. Christopher, the patron saint of travelers, asking him to intercede with God on our behalf that we may arrive and return safely from our field trip to Cleveland Public Hall."

"St. Christopher," Sister Magdalene began reverently.

"Pray for us," the class responded enthusiastically.

With that, Mr. Kinderly cranked the engine of the yellow school bus, accelerated gently, and they were on their way.

For weeks, Jimmy had been waiting for this day to arrive. Although it was only mid-February and he still had plenty of time to write his essay, he was worried. He simply could not think of where to begin. *As a seventh grader, what can I contribute to the space program?* This was the theme of the contest. It seemed simple enough. Most of the boys would probably say they wanted to be astronauts. As for the girls, possibly working for NASA as secretaries was a choice or even marrying an astronaut and being a stay-at-home wife. Not much imagination in any case. But not Jimmy. He wanted something different and unique. But what? He was stuck. Hopefully, today's visit to the exhibition would give him some ideas.

Halfway through the ride to Cleveland, a chant began to emerge from the back of the bus:

"Old MacDonald had a farm. E-I-E-I-O.
And on that farm he had a pig. E-I-E-I-O.
With an oink oink here.
And an oink oink there.
Here an oink.
There an oink.
Everywhere an oink oink.
Old MacDonald had a farm. E-I-E-I-O.
Old MacDonald had a farm. E-I-E-I-O.
And on that farm he had a duck . . ."

By the time the bus rolled up to the entrance of Cleveland Public Hall on Lakeside Avenue the class had acknowledged practically every animal imagined and then some . . . snake, antelope, lizard, buffalo. Even a dinosaur.

Before Mr. Kinderly opened the door of the bus, Sister Mary Magdalene stood up and addressed the class. "Remember students, that you are representing St. Rita School. There will be no running, shouting, or fighting while you are in the exhibition. Failure to abide by the rules means a visit to our principal, Sister Mary Celeste. And you know what that means. Do I make myself clear, Mr. Drabek?"

"Oh yes, Sister," replied Dennis angelically.

"Don't let Magdalene's habit fool you," Lee whispered to Jimmy, "she knows who the class troublemaker is.

For Jimmy, the Project Mercury exhibition was simply out of this world. It paid tribute to the astronauts, the engineers and the innovators who dreamed the dream of someday going to the moon and beyond. Illustrated text panels and photo blowups highlighting key moments in the history of the NASA space program dotted the galleries. Exhibit halls offered everything from spacecraft parts and astronaut suits to working launch consoles. A special exhibit was dedicated to Ham, the first chimpanzee to be launched into space from Cape Canaveral in Florida just two weeks earlier on January 31. Ham had been trained to pull levers to receive rewards of banana pellets and avoid electric shocks. His flight demonstrated the ability to perform tasks during spaceflight.

"How neat is that?" shouted Jimmy as he and Lee ran up

to the Ham exhibit. "A monkey in space!" Soon more classmates, including Terri, gathered about the two boys to see what all the excitement was about.

"Hi, Jimmy," greeted Terri cheerfully. "Feel like Tom Corbett today?"

"I sure do Terri. I am almost halfway through reading *On the Trail of the Space Pirates,* the third book in the series. It's a thousand times more thrilling than any story of pirates on the high seas or the Spanish Main." Terri was glad for Jimmy. She knew how much he wanted to win Sister Mary Magdalene's essay contest.

"Well, if it isn't Flash Gordon and his girlfriend Dale." Jimmy not only recognized the reference to the comic strip space hero but the voice behind it. Striding menacingly towards him and Terri was Dennis Drabek with Praser and Shorts in his wake.

"Why don't you make like a tree and leave," said Terri.

"You're a real riot aren't you," Dennis sneered. "Too bad NASA is not sending up a mouse into space, Jimmy would be the perfect candidate.

"Well, you definitely wouldn't qualify," countered Terri. "With a fat pig like you, the rocket would never get off the ground!"

"Yesssssss," shouted Lee. "Way to go Terri!"

With that Terri asked Lee if he would not mind swapping seats with her on the ride back to St. Rita

School.

"Sure will," said Lee.

"You're the best," Terri replied thankfully as she made her way to the bus.

"Listen, Jimmy," said Terri, "Drabek is nothing but a brat and everyone knows it. Do not let him distract you from what you really want. Keep focused on Sister Magdalene's essay contest." Before Jimmy could reply, she reached into the pocket of her winter jacket and pulled out a red envelope. "Here, Jimmy," she said. "From me to you."

Jimmy was puzzled. "What's this?"

"Don't you know what day it is tomorrow?" asked Terri.

"Sure, it's Thursday."

"No, silly, it's Valentines' Day!"

Jimmy's face turned as red as the envelope.

"Will you be my Valentine?" whispered Terri softly.

Jimmy opened the envelope, read the card then reached over and gently held her hand.

Chapter 11

Jimmy and Elaine

Jimmy struggled to pull his black rubber boots over his shoes. Once secured, he tucked in his jeans then snapped into place the five metal clasps running vertically along the front of each boot. He reached in the front door closet for his heavy brown corduroy jacket then jumped a foot or two to snag the matching earflap hat lying on the shelf just above the hangars. The weather in Solon was cold and blustery.

Jimmy was all but willing to brave the snowy weather. He and Doll were on their way to 'the corner' to spend snow shoveling money on comic books at Rexall Pharmacy. Plus, it was Saturday morning. What could be better than that?

"How about this," Doll shouted to Jimmy above the blowing wind. "Elaine is working behind the soda fountain today. Maybe she can sneak us a cherry Coke and even a pretzel rod when Mr. Knapp is not looking."

"You really think your sister will risk losing her job for you? The two of you are always arguing with each other. No way!"

"Well, I'm going to try anyhow!" snapped Doll with determination.

Jimmy could only shake his head. "Step it up, I'm getting cold!"

The boys stomped their boots twice, knocking off snow and slush before walking into the pharmacy. Immediately they zeroed in on the spinning vertical comic book rack just beyond the double-tiered magazine stand to their right. The clacking of Mr. Knapp's typewriter was an ever-present beat.

A smorgasbord of comic book titles greeted them at every turn of the rack. *Archie, Little Lulu, Superman, The Lone Ranger, Tales from the Crypt, Katy Keene.* But it was a copy of *Strange Worlds* that made Jimmy's eyes pop. "I was the first victim of a *MANHUNT ON MARS!*" the cover shouted back at him. The illustration of a spaceman crouching fearfully behind a fractured Martian outcropping attempting to elude a platoon of green-headed alien beings moving towards him was too much to resist. "That's it," he erupted, "that's the one!"

Mr. Knapp quickly looked up his concentration interrupted for the moment. "Everything all right Jimmy?" he inquired.

"Sorry, Mr. Knapp, this new comic book about astronauts on Mars looks so cool. I'll be over in a few minutes to pay you for it."

"I'm glad you're excited, Jimmy. Take your time."

Doll, unlike Jimmy, had no interest in outer space. "I've got what I came for," he said, flashing a *Kid Colt Outlaw* comic book in Jimmy's face. "You can have your stories about astronauts and little green men, I'll take blazing six-guns any day."

"Whatever," responded Jimmy. "Let's pay for our comic books then head to the soda fountain."

"Hey guys," greeted Elaine cheerfully, "what can I get for you?"

"A cherry Coke, please," said Jimmy.

"Of course, good choice." Elaine turned to Doll. "What about you squirt?"

"Mom told you not to call me that, Elaine!"

"What would you like . . . sir?" Elaine smirked.

"I'll have a pretzel rod and a cherry Coke."

"Oh, I'll have a pretzel rod also," continued Jimmy.

"Two cherry Cokes coming right up and two pretzel rods not far behind," kidded Elaine.

"Oh, by the way, Jimmy, how did your class visit to Public Hall go on Wednesday?"

"It was great. I'm so excited about the possibilities of exploring outer space someday."

"Sounds pretty boring to me," chimed in Doll.

"Boring?" Elaine shook her head disapprovingly at her brother's remark.

"To make things worse," Doll shot back, "Sister Mary Magdalene is forcing Jimmy's class to write an essay about space."

"Well, it's more like a contest," said Jimmy. "Every student is to write an essay themed *as a seventh grader what can I contribute to the space program*? We have until the end of the school year to complete it."

Doll butted in, "And the only prize the winner gets is a stupid book about the Mercury astronauts. Why can't they get a pocketknife or gun holster? How about a refill, Elaine?"

Elaine sighed, "I can't put up with your stupid remarks anymore, squirt. I have customers to attend to. That will be ten cents for the Cokes and two cents for the pretzel rods. Thank you, Jimmy, have a fun day."

"Okay Elaine, bye."

"Come on, Jimmy," said Doll, "let's go over to my house to play a game."

Elaine turned to wipe off the marble-top counter of the soda fountain. There it was, lying on top; Jimmy's *Strange Worlds* comic book. The boys had already left Rexall. She would return it to him after work.

Jimmy was on the attack. For the last three hours, late into the afternoon, he and Doll sat at the kitchen table in the Shiver house. They were locked in mortal combat both concealing, bluffing, lying in wait. The Napoleonic

Wars had come to Solon. The game was *Stratego*. It was one of Doll's Christmas gifts straight from the North Pole.

"Gotcha," shouted Jimmy triumphantly, as his Spy moved in to capture Doll's Marshall. Chomping on a Ruffles potato chip loaded with French onion dip, he sensed victory.

As Doll struggled to reclaim his advantage, Elaine, just home from work, walked into the room. "Oh, hi Jimmy! Here, you left your *Strange Worlds* comic book at Rexall."

"Oh my gosh, thanks, Elaine! I was so focused on whipping the pants off Doll in *Stratego* I didn't even notice it was gone."

Elaine paused, "The comic book was really interesting."

"You read my comic book?" a surprised Jimmy responded. "I didn't know girls read comic books."

"It was really good. I could hardly put it down during my break. I'm so fascinated by outer space."

"Sister Mary Magdalene told us the Soviet Union is thinking of sending a man into space soon."

"I know, I heard it from Mr. Sheffield too, it's wild! I would just love to orbit around the planets, seeing them right there in front of me."

"I've got more comic books about space if you'd like to read them," offered Jimmy enthusiastically.

"Sure!"

Doll looked up from the game board, first at Jimmy then at Elaine, "You two are nerds," was all he could say.

Chapter 12

Mildred and Elaine

Elaine lay casually across her bed thumbing through an issue of *Teen* magazine. "Frankie's Flame Won't Flicker" the cover story promised as a dreamy Frankie Avalon smiled back at the reader. Neatly cutout pictures of music and film stars from a variety of magazines were taped randomly to the wall behind her bed. Ricky, Fabian, Sandra, Troy, Annette and, of course, Frankie. The magazines were compliments of Mr. Knapp, a perk for working the soda fountain at Rexall Pharmacy. A plush brown teddy bear named Boopsie lounged between Elaine's two pillows while Amelia, a furry pink elephant, loafed nearby. Jules Verne's *From the Earth to the Moon* sat open on her nightstand partially overlapping *Mystery in Space*, one of Jimmy's comic books. A 45 dropped from a stack of records onto the turntable of Elaine's Crosley Dansette Junior record player.

"*Dream, dream, dream, dream*
Dream, dream, dream, dream

When I want you in my arms
When I want you and all your . . ."

BANG!!

The sweet harmony of the Everly Brothers was shattered as Elaine's mother threw open her bedroom door unannounced, the doorknob slamming into the wall, leaving a dent. Mildred stood over her daughter glaring. "Can you explain this?" she demanded, Elaine's essay from Mr. Sheffield clutched in her hand.

"It's my paper on what to expect in the future," replied Elaine sitting up abruptly.

Arms now folded to match her stern face, Mildred snapped, "I know what it is. You should be ashamed of yourself. A grade of D, Elaine?"

"Ashamed of myself?" Elaine was incredulous. "I can't believe you're saying that. Look, I wrote what I knew to be true. What I felt the future will hold. Did you even read it?"

Mildred's voice escalated, "Of course, I read it. It was supposed to be a paper about facts not fiction, not 'time will only tell what the future holds for us. Men and women will be on the same level of understanding and not one ahead of the other.' Where did you get such an idea?"

Elaine stared at her mother, unrepentant, "I can't believe you're siding with Mr. Sheffield."

Impatient with her daughter's unwillingness to give in, Mildred shouted defiantly, "You will do dishes every night this week." Turning abruptly, she stalked out of Elaine's bedroom satisfied she had the final say.

Frustrated, Elaine fell back on the bed. "Oh, I get it," she said sarcastically, "put her back in the kitchen where she belongs."

The next 45 record quietly dropped to the turntable and began to play.

Chapter 13

Mildred and Mae

Mildred Shiver slowly pushed her shopping cart up and down the aisles of Sargent's grocery store. Her head swiveled from left to right then right to left carefully searching the shelves for the items of food her family would require for the upcoming week: pork chops, a roast, hot dogs, Swanson TV dinners, Cheerios, Wonder Bread, Sealtest ice cream (vanilla), two six-packs of Stroh's beer for her husband Ed, and much more. As she wound her way to the check-out counter, Mildred spotted Mae Ryan standing thoughtfully in front of the dairy section. She had not seen Mae since the last bridge club get-together some weeks ago.

"Hi, Mae," she called out to her neighbor.

"Oh! Hi, Mildred," Mae turned to respond. "How are you?"

"Just trying to get a jump on the day. More chores to do at home, you know."

As the two women engaged in small talk for a moment, Mildred unexpectedly fell silent, a worried expression spreading across her face like a sad mask.

"Mildred, what's wrong?" a concerned Mae inquired.

"I'm Okay, Mae, it's nothing." Then suddenly. "Well, it's just that . . ."

Mae was puzzled. "Just what, Mildred? Please tell me."

Uncharacteristically, Mildred blurted out, an edge in the tone of her voice. "Just what do you and the girls from the bridge club think of Elaine?"

"What do you mean? We all think highly of Elaine," Mae responded.

Mildred became tearful. "I just don't know what to do with her, Mae. She is so different, and always challenging me. Your daughter, Peggy, seems so prim and proper, always doing what is expected of a young girl. I'm just confused and embarrassed by Elaine's behavior."

"Well, fourteen is a tough age," offered Mae. "Do you think Elaine is just as confused and frustrated as you?"

"How would I know? I simply do not understand her!"

"Hmmmm, perhaps you are both trying to understand the same thing but from different places." Without warning, Mildred abruptly ended the conversation. "I need to run now, Mae," she said with some urgency. "Ed has a golf date at noon, and I have to get home to fix his lunch."

Mae was left standing speechless.

Mildred checked out quickly and made her way to the

family Ford station wagon in Sargent's parking lot. Ed was waiting in the driver's seat reading the sport's page.

"Mae was just being kind. I know they all think Elaine is rebellious. Well, let them talk," she said defiantly to herself. "Elaine is *my* daughter! As my mother taught me to be the proper wife and caretaker of my children and to know my place as a homemaker, so I will also raise Elaine as I see fit." She hastily tossed the grocery bags into the back seat of the car and slammed the door in frustration.

"Get everything you need?" Ed asked casually.

Mildred sat silently as the Ford headed for home, slightly turning her head to the right as to hide a tear slowly welling up, yet too small to roll down her face.

Chapter 14

Strat-O-Flier

March was a windy month in Solon. Jimmy sat Indian style on his bedroom floor. Balls of crumbled paper torn from his Big Chief writing tablet were strewn about. Write, tear, crumble. Write, tear, crumble. An idea for Sister Mary Magdalene's essay contest was simply not coming to him. A sentence or two hastily put to paper in a burst of inspiration was just as quickly torn and discarded. Jimmy was frustrated. He was determined to win the book about the Mercury astronauts. He knew most of his classmates would be writing about becoming astronauts as their contribution to the space program. Jimmy also dreamed of traveling in outer space, but he wanted something different from his friends, something out of this world. But what? The wind rattled his bedroom window. Jimmy put down his writing tablet, grabbed his kite tucked in a corner of the bedroom next to his bookshelf, and walked outside. He needed a break.

Jimmy's backyard was too small for kite flying. Instead, he walked across the street toward the Eagleton's house, cut through their backyard, and wandered into the large cornfield that lay just beyond. There was plenty of room for flying a kite in the open field this time of year before corn planting in late spring. Jimmy's kite was a classic two-stick diamond bow made by the Hi-Flier Kite Company. On the front at the top, the words Strat-O-Flier in red letters trimmed in gold arced across a blue sky while a futuristic rocket, angled diagonally against a yellow sun, shot through the middle. Below were the words Hi-Flier in red.

The sky was a bit overcast, but the robust wind was perfect. Jimmy had no problem getting his kite up in the air. Once airborne, he gently pumped the string, increasing the altitude. For more lift, he pulled in the line a few feet and then slowly let it out. As Jimmy began to think once more about his essay, he lost sight of the fact that his kite was climbing higher and higher in the sky, the ball of string quickly unraveling. Suddenly he felt a jolt in his hands as the kite string became taut as a drumhead. His concentration broken; Jimmy looked up. The kite was practically a pinpoint in the sky. He never dreamed it could rise that high, never dared to use an entire ball of string for fear it would snap, and the kite would be lost. Yet there it was, practically on the fringe of outer space. Suddenly, he noticed the wind had picked up significantly, the air was becoming cooler and dark thunderclouds were moving in overhead.

"Oh, Jimmy! Jimmy! Time to come home for dinner," shouted Marge Dixon from across the street.

"Oh, great," Jimmy thought to himself, "I'll be there in a few minutes, Mom."

Jimmy struggled to pull in his kite against the resistance of the strong wind. It was simply taking too much time. His mom would be angry if he did not come right away. Spotting a wooden stick lying on the ground, he picked it up, jammed it into the soil of the field, wrapped the end of the kite string around the stick, tied it with a double knot then turned and ran home. He would come back for the kite after dinner.

Mrs. Dixon had prepared meatloaf with scalloped potatoes and cut green beans for her family. Although meatloaf was one of Jimmy's favorite meals, he hardly noticed. Large claps of thunder rumbled outside with fierce lightning illuminating the sky. Wind rattled the windows. Then the rains came.

"Something wrong, Jimmy?" inquired his father, Ted.

"No, nothing Dad, the meatloaf's great."

"Mom made a nice grasshopper pie for dessert," chimed in Jimmy's sister Barb.

"Oh, okay!"

"Don't sound too enthusiastic," Ted joked.

"Sorry, Dad, it's just that my kite is still up in the air behind Eagleton's house and with this storm, who knows?"

"Don't worry, son; when the storm clears, you can go back for your kite. Now finish your dinner."

The storm came and went. Dusk began to settle over Solon.

Jimmy raced out of the house and sprinted for the cornfield. Drawing closer he spotted the wooden stick raised vertically from the ground, upright as he left it, also the string. A very limp string going nowhere. Although he already knew the fate of his kite, a victim of the storm, Jimmy scanned the sky as if the Strat-O-Flier would somehow miraculously appear from behind a cloud. After a few minutes he turned and slowly walked back home.

That night, as Jimmy lay in bed, he realized he still had no idea what to write for the essay contest.

Chapter 15

Elaine and Mr. Sheffield

Elaine moved her index finger slowly across the large map of American Civil War battlefields which hung on the wall just to the left of Mr. Sheffield's desk. In an open notebook nestled in the crook of her arm, she jotted information about the Battle of Shiloh, fought in southwestern Tennessee. The classroom was empty. All the students had left for the day. *"Only one more battle site, and I'll be finished,"* she thought to herself. As Elaine began searching for the location of the Gettysburg battlefield, Mr. Sheffield walked into the classroom unexpectantly.

"You're still here?" he inquired. "You do know what day this is don't you, Miss Shiver?"

"Yes sir, Monday. I was just finishing up some homework."

"Well, they call it homework for a reason Miss Shiver," quipped Mr. Sheffield.

"Yes sir, I know," Elaine acknowledged quietly.

Mr. Sheffield pursed his lips slightly. Elaine had always

presented herself as a bit of a free spirit, he thought, very much her own person and certainly not always in agreement with him in class. He then opened the middle drawer of his desk, pulled out an envelope and handed it to Elaine. "Here, give this to your mother," was all he said.

Puzzled, Elaine reached for the envelope, "What is this?"

"Your mother asked that I start sending home a weekly progress report of how you're doing in my class."

Elaine was taken aback, "Oh! thank you," was all she could respond. Her face a hurt mask, she wandered over to her desk to gather her books. Mr. Sheffield, now seated and grading papers, paid no attention as his student walked silently past him to exit the classroom.

Suddenly, Elaine paused at the door and turned toward her teacher. "Mr. Sheffield, can I ask you a question?"

Mr. Sheffield looked up from his desk. "Why sure, Elaine, what is it?"

"Do you think they'll ever send a female into space?"

Mr. Sheffield grinned sarcastically, "Miss Shiver, a woman's place is in the home. Better leave space flight to the men," he said with amusement.

Elaine walked out of the classroom without responding.

Chapter 16

The Astronaut

"The Observatory of Cambridge, in its memorable letter, had treated the question from a purely astronomical point . . ." Elaine had just begun Chapter Four of Jules Verne's *From the Earth to the Moon* when the doorbell rang at the Shiver home. Jumping off the couch, she was surprised to see Jimmy framed in the doorway.

"Oh, hey Jimmy," she said.

"Hi, Elaine, do you have some time to walk across the street to the cornfield behind Eagleton's house? I need your help with something."

"Sure Jimmy, let me grab a sweater, it's still a bit chilly outside even for late April."

As the pair approached the cornfield, Elaine spotted a kite flying in the sky, its string staked to a piece of wood in the ground.

"It's my new kite," Jimmy said, anticipating a question from Elaine. "Another Strat-O-Flier to replace my old one which I lost in a storm in March. I had to shovel quite a few driveways to buy it."

"So, what did you need help with?" questioned Elaine.

"For my essay," Jimmy explained, "I want to get my kite higher than it has gone before, even higher than the day the storm snapped my kite string. You know, to see how close I can get to outer space. I want it to be my rocket ship."

Elaine looked up at the Strat-O-Flier her eyes squinting from the sun's glare. "But don't you need an astronaut to send up in space?" she wondered.

"Yeah, I've been thinking about that all day, but nothing's come to me."

"That would be more impressive than just seeing a kite go up."

"Yeah, but what can we use?" thought Jimmy.

Elaine chuckled pointing to the sky. "We're too big to fit on that kite. We need something that can act as a guinea pig. But what?" she hesitated.

Jimmy paused, then in a burst of inspiration shouted, "DRABEK, the Project Mercury exhibition! He called me a mouse. I've got an idea Elaine, come on!" Grabbing her by the hand, he sprinted to the woods which rimmed the far end of the cornfield.

As they approached the trees Elaine stopped suddenly nearly yanking her neighbor to the ground. "Wait a minute, Jimmy," she exclaimed, "what on Earth are we looking for? And what was that about Dennis Drabek?"

Jimmy walked slowly towards Elaine and whispered in her ear as if fearful the Soviet space agency would steal his secret.

"Wow, that's it!" she shouted. "No time to waste, let's start looking."

Jimmy and Elaine silently began searching the woods, cautiously avoiding the crunch of fallen leaves or the snap of dead branches.

"Do you think we can get on the Ed Sullivan Show for this?"

"Let's worry about your essay first," Elaine advised.

"Well, if José Jiménez can get on the show just for saying his name, I think we have a chance."

"I love when he does that," Elaine chuckled as she mimicked her best impersonation, "My name . . . José Jiménez."

"Yeah, my name . . . José Jiménez," repeated Jimmy his searching eyes never leaving the ground. "Gotcha!"

Elaine turned quickly to see Jimmy kneeling on the ground his cupped hands cradled to his jacket. Peeking out at her from a small hole formed by his thumb and forefinger was a field mouse. "Our astronaut," Jimmy proclaimed triumphantly.

"Good work."

"What now?" asked Jimmy.

"We need to build some sort of device to attach to the kite to send him up. Before that, however, our astronaut will require some physical training. I can help you with that in a few days after he gets used to being with us for a while."

"He can stay at my house," volunteered Jimmy. "Our parakeet Sydney's old cage is down in the basement. Mom's been meaning to throw it out. Come on little buddy," Jimmy whispered to his astronaut, "I'll take you to Cape Dixon."

Back home, Elaine's mom was furious.

"A mouse, Elaine?" Mildred's frustration was evident. "Seriously?"

Elaine could only shake her head. "You just don't get it do you Mom? I have told you time and time again how interested I am in outer space and want to be an astronaut someday. I'm determined to help Jimmy Dixon with his school project no matter what you say."

"Well, I can only pray that this wild notion of yours disappears soon and you will come to your senses."

Chapter 17

Mr. Tagger

Jimmy had been pacing outside Tagger's Pet Shop for the last twenty minutes waiting for the store to open at 9:00 am. "Come on clock, faster," he urged. Soon he was rewarded by the click of the door lock and the smiling face of Henry Tagger standing just inside the entrance.

"Good morning Jimmy," the store owner said, "early bird catches the worm, right? What can I help you with today . . . dog food, cat litter? Perhaps a friendly snake to cuddle with?"

Jimmy laughed. "Hi, Mr. Tagger. Actually mice."

"Oh, you want to purchase a mouse. I have a few Chinese mice towards the back of the store. They make wonderful pets, very friendly. Cute."

"I don't want to buy a mouse, I have one, but I do need some mouse stuff."

"Mouse stuff?" Mr. Tagger was puzzled.

"You know, mouse food, toys, things like that."

"Oh, I see," said Mr. Tagger nodding, "mouse stuff. Hmmmm, not the usual request, but let us see what I can do for you. Grab a cart Jimmy and follow me."

The storekeeper walked toward the back of his shop stopping about halfway down the second aisle. "First you need a cage," he suggested.

"Well, my mouse is now living in our old bird cage," explained Jimmy.

"Sorry, that won't do," said Mr. Tagger. "A bird cage is simply too small to hold all your mouse stuff." The storekeeper removed a cage from the shelf and placed it into Jimmy's cart. "This should do nicely," he said. Next came a food dish, then a drip bottle, then a small squeaky toy, a clear plastic bag filled with wood shavings for bedding, an exercise wheel, and finally a hidey hole for resting in.

"Whoa, hold on Mr. Tagger!" interrupted Jimmy. He looked worried. "How much is all of my mouse stuff going to cost?"

The shopkeeper paused for a moment then smiled. "Tell you what, Jimmy," he said. "Now that summer is almost upon us you can pay me a little at a time with money earned from mowing your dad's lawn and washing his car."

"Gee, thanks, Mr. Tagger," Jimmy shouted, "you're the best. Actually, I do have some snow shoveling money saved up which I can pay you right now for starters."

"That would be fine. Now one more thing. Your

mouse needs to eat, right? Here is a bag of mouse food. Also, have your mom chop up some fresh fruit and vegetables. Your pet will love you for it."

"By the way, Jimmy," Mr. Tagger inquired. "Just what do you plan to do with your mouse? Simply keep him as a pet?"

"Far from it, Mr. Tagger, I'm sending my mouse into outer space and maybe even to the moon someday," proclaimed Jimmy enthusiastically!

"Well, there will certainly be plenty of green cheese for him to feast on when he gets there," laughed Henry Tagger.

"Thanks again Mr. Tagger," shouted Jimmy, as he sprinted out the pet shop door clutching two full bags of mouse stuff, one under each arm.

Chapter 18

Shepard

Jimmy sat quietly in his St. Rita classroom waiting for the Friday morning announcements. Although it was nearly a week since he and Elaine had discovered the field mouse in the woods, he could think of nothing else but his furry astronaut, not even Little League practice beginning soon. School would be over on June 2 and Jimmy had yet to complete his essay due in about three weeks. Time was running out. This weekend he and Elaine would begin preparing the mouse for its future launch.

Jimmy's concentration was broken by the crackling of his classroom's PA system. The familiar voice of Sister Mary Celeste filled the room. "Good morning students," the school's principal said. "Before my morning announcements, I have a special surprise for you all. As some of you may be aware, America will be sending its first astronaut into space today. The launch from Cape Canaveral in Florida is expected at 9:30 am about an hour from now. At that time, we will turn on the radio to ABC News, so that you will be able to hear a live broadcast of this historic event in your classrooms. I will now lead you in a prayer for astronaut Alan B. Shepard asking God in His mercy to keep him safe during his flight."

"I can't believe it," thought Jimmy, "this is perfect timing." Nearly three weeks before, on April 12, the stakes were raised in the space race when Soviet cosmonaut Yuri Gagarin became the first person to orbit the Earth. Gagarin beat the Americans into space by less than a month. Shepard's launch was initially scheduled for May 2 but was rescheduled twice because of weather conditions. Jimmy was sure he could get some really good ideas for his essay today. After much anticipation, the countdown blared from the classroom's PA box as Sister Mary Magdalene's class sat transfixed.

"T Minus 10 9 8 7 6 5 4 3 2 1 0 . . . ignition . . . lift off, lift off at thirty-four minutes after the hour."

For the next forty seconds the roar from the Mercury-Redstone rocket rumbled through the classroom. Jimmy could not take a breath.

"Trajectory looks A-OK, pitch control A-OK, switching to manual yaw . . . medical monitoring in Mercury control reports pilot's condition appears to be excellent . . . Freedom 7 in voice control with the Mercury control center." Jimmy's class cheered wildly.

Shepard's Mercury capsule, designated Freedom 7,

carried the American astronaut to an altitude of 116 miles. His historic flight lasted 15 minutes, 28 seconds before splashing down in the Atlantic Ocean 302 miles from the Florida launch site.

As the radio broadcast faded away, Sister Mary Celeste's voice came over the PA once more. "Students, in celebration of America's successful first flight into space, Monsignor Mazer and I have decided to cancel classes for the rest of the day with no homework assigned. Have a wonderful weekend!"

Jimmy could hardly sleep that night. Tomorrow his space adventure would begin with all systems go!

Chapter 19

Bartlett

Jimmy's mouse lay sound asleep, nestled in the wood shavings of his cage. "Rise and shine," shouted Jimmy as he drew back his covers and sprang from his bed.

It was seven o' clock in the morning. Most Saturdays even an atomic explosion could not budge Jimmy from a deep sleep before noon. But today was different.

"Training begins at 0800. Elaine will be here soon. Up and at 'em."

The field mouse raised its sleepy head, yawned slightly, then burrowed deeper into the comfort zone of the wood shavings.

"Okay, Okay," said Jimmy. "You can sleep a little longer while I go downstairs for breakfast."

No sooner had Jimmy reached the bottom of the stairs then the front doorbell rang. It was Elaine.

"Good morning, Jimmy. All set to begin our adventure?"

"You bet," he responded with excitement. "Mom is making breakfast. Let's eat quickly and then get our astronaut."

"Whoa, hold on! Let's not disturb him just yet," chuckled Elaine. "He will need all his energy this morning when we begin his physical training."

Jimmy agreed. "Let's go into our garage and begin building his capsule to be attached to the kite for his flight into space. My dad helped me pick out some of the materials yesterday at Solon Hardware."

"So, how's your essay coming along?" inquired Elaine as they walked to the garage after a hearty breakfast of scrambled eggs, bacon, and toast.

"Ehhh! Not so good," admitted Jimmy.

"How come? I thought you knew what you wanted to write about."

"I do, but I just don't know how to begin, how to put it down on paper."

"Maybe I can help you," suggested Elaine. "When did you first become interested in space?"

Jimmy paused thoughtfully for a moment. "Well, actually when Sister Mary Magdalene first taught our class about the Mercury astronauts." A wide smile then came across his face. "But I *really* became interested when Terri Lloyd gave me the first Tom Corbett, Space Cadet book as a surprise Christmas gift last December."

"Well, there you go," said Elaine to a slightly blushing Jimmy. "Write about how both Sister *and* Terri first got you interested in space and take it from there."

"Yeah, okay, that's a start," Jimmy nodded in agreement.

"See, you know what you want to write, you just had to think about it."

As Elaine began sketching designs for the kite's capsule to be constructed with popsicle sticks, wire and glue, Jimmy turned to her inquiring, "So, what do you want to name our new astronaut?"

"Hmmmm," thought Elaine. "You know, I feel the name should symbolize someone or something in the space program."

"How about Sputnik?" Jimmy offered.

Elaine shook her head. "No, too Russian . . . Pioneer?"

"Nah, too used." Then suddenly . . . "Alan?"

"Oh, as in Alan B. Shepard?"

"Yeah, that's it," Jimmy acknowledged.

"You know, that's not a bad idea, but why don't we call him after Shepard's middle name," suggested Elaine.

Jimmy was puzzled. "You want to name him B?"

"Bartlett! You will learn that next year in your eighth-grade science class."

"Bartlett!" Jimmy grinned. "Yeah, Bartlett!"

Elaine poked Jimmy. "Come on, we have a lot to do before astronaut Bartlett wakes up."

A half hour later, Jimmy and Elaine were ready to begin Bartlett's first astronaut-in-training session.

"You okay, Jimmy?" Elaine inquired looking up.

"Almost there, Elaine," Jimmy replied, a bit out of breath. He had been moving steadily towards the top of a tall tree step by step and branch by branch. Slung across his shoulder was a large coil of rope. Attached to one end of the rope was a small cage, a test capsule for Bartlett. The tree was one of a group of black maples which lay at the edge of the cornfield just beyond Eagleton's house. As the leaves of the maple were just beginning to bud in early May the climb up for Jimmy was easy. In fact, he had made it many times. Sailing the "Seven Seas," the tree was Jimmy's route to the crow's nest in search of marauding pirate ships. While on safari in the Congo he climbed to its highest branch to safely escape the wrath of a charging Rhino.

Jimmy learned from Sister Magdalene's lesson on the Mercury Seven that astronaut training was a complex process. It was geared to the special conditions and environments confronting astronauts during a launch in space, and during landing. Bartlett's daily schedule included a fifteen- minute workout on his exercise wheel. "He must be physically fit," stressed Elaine. Crawling through a cardboard paper towel tube three times a day prepared him for the enclosed space of the capsule in which he would be confined during the flight. To maintain his strength a daily meal of barley and millet was offered plus a balance of broccoli, carrots, and celery, the crunchier the better. A piece of apple was served as a healthy treat, and always fresh water.

"Just about," Jimmy called down to Elaine. As he reached the final branch of his climb he turned and braced his back against the trunk of the tree. Jimmy tied one end of the rope to the branch and then slowly lowered the cage down to Elaine waiting below. As the cage gently touched the ground, she lovingly reached into a small wooden box carefully lifting Bartlett from the wood shavings upon which he lay. On Elaine's signal that the astronaut-in-training was securely inside, Jimmy began pulling the cage upward to the branch upon which he stood some twenty feet above the ground. Bartlett's short ride was meant to test his reaction to flying above the Earth in an enclosed space. Both Jimmy and Elaine hoped this experience would prepare him adequately for his much longer and higher flight.

For this first attempt, Jimmy lifted the cage slowly and steadily skyward to avoid frightening Bartlett during his initial venture off the ground. In two days, he would not be so forgiving as this phase of training would be repeated a second time. The plan was to swing the cage from time to time to mimic the movement of the Strat-O-Flier buffeted by occasional gusts of wind. "But first things first," thought Jimmy as he nervously awaited the arrival of Bartlett. As the cage drew closer, he reached out, grabbed the rope, and swung the capsule toward him.

"How is he?" shouted Elaine anxiously.

"Hahahahah," laughed Jimmy. "He fell asleep. I guess the ride was a relaxing one."

"Oh, that crazy mouse," chuckled Elaine. "Mission accomplished."

Back in Jimmy's room after a day's training, Bartlett showing little interest in snacking on a grape crawled into his hidey hole and was soon fast asleep.

Chapter 20

Confrontation

When Mr. Sheffield walked into his classroom at the end of the school day, he was surprised to see Elaine still working at her desk. "Miss Shiver," he called to her with some impatience.

Elaine looked up attentively. "Sorry, sir," she said quietly, "I was just finishing some homework."

"Yes, but school ended fifteen minutes ago. Usually on Friday afternoon most of the students run out the door as soon as the bell rings."

Elaine hesitated for a moment then exclaimed in a challenging tone, "You're wrong, you know!"

Mr. Sheffield was taken aback. "I beg your pardon?"

"Saying that a woman will never go into space." Elaine responded.

"Not that rubbish again!" he countered.

Elaine looked Mr. Sheffield straight in the eye. "How can *you*, a man of history, have such a narrow way of thinking?"

Now he was obviously frustrated at her attitude. "Face the

facts, Miss Shiver, there has never been a woman in space and there never will be. They will more likely send another monkey before they send a woman."

"Well, *I'm going*," said Elaine.

"Going where, Miss Shiver?"

"Up in space," she proclaimed with determination while gathering her books to leave.

"When?" he shrugged.

"In the future," Elaine countered.

Mr. Sheffield could only sigh and shake his head.

As Elaine approached the classroom door she hesitated, then turned to face her teacher. "Change is happening all around us Mr. Sheffield, you can choose to ignore it or embrace it. *Your choice!*"

The room became silent. Elaine entered the hallway and walked past the lockers.

Mr. Sheffield was at a loss for words.

Chapter 21

And the winner is...

St. Rita School playground was in full tilt. The bell had just rung for recess and most students, after wolfing down their lunches, were out the front door like a herd of cattle. Girls skipped rope and hopscotched. Some boys brought their gloves to school and played catch. Others played Red Rover or climbed the monkey bars. Yet the bell to end recess could not have come soon enough for Jimmy. It was Wednesday of the second to last week of class before summer vacation. For Jimmy, the prospect of a three-month respite from school was just fine. But today was different. As soon as he and his classmates returned to their room Sister Mary Magdalene would announce the winner of the Project Mercury essay contest. He was nervous but satisfied he had done the very best he could. Bartlett, Elaine, Tom Corbett, Sister Magdalene, even Ham the chimpanzee, all were contributors to his venture.

"Please be seated class," asked Sister Magdalene. Once settled, the students listened attentively. "Last December I introduced you to NASA and the Project Mercury space program. Since that time, many of you have been working diligently on your contest essays answering the question *what can I as a seventh grader contribute to the space program?* Today I am happy to announce the contest winner. It was a very difficult decision as there were so many excellent submissions. In fact, I recruited both Sister Mary Cecilia and Sister Mary Annunciata as additional readers. Some of you wrote that you wanted to be astronauts while others dreamed of building rocket ships for NASA. One of you even hoped to become a millionaire someday and pay for the first mission to Mars. Very creative! Yet, one essay stood out among all the rest and for a very good reason which I will explain to you momentarily. But first, the winner of the Project Mercury essay contest." Sister Magdalene paused for a moment then smiled. "Jimmy Dixon, please come to the front of the room," she said. The classroom exploded with cheers. Dennis Drabek glared caustically.

Jimmy could hardly contain himself as he practically ran to the front of the classroom. A wink from Terri and a grin from Lee brought him back to Earth. "Congratulations, Jimmy," said Sister Magdalene as she handed him the prize for first place, a book about the Mercury astronauts. "Thank you, Sister," replied Jimmy respectfully. Then he turned and whispered something to her. She nodded and smiled.

Once Jimmy returned to his seat Sister Mary Magdalene explained to the class why his essay was chosen. "Jimmy's essay was special," she said. "He felt the best way to contribute to the space program was to actually *experience* the space program. How does NASA choose its astronauts? How are astronauts trained? What do they eat? How is an astronaut launched into space? For Jimmy, the solution was unique. He not only chose his own astronaut but trained him and fed him and will soon send him into space. The astronaut, whose name is Bartlett, is a field mouse that Jimmy caught in the woods not too far from his house. The exciting news is that he will be launching Bartlett into the sky next Wednesday, two days before the end of the school year. On his kite. Yes, Bartlett will ride into space in a special cage, his capsule, which will be attached to Jimmy's kite."

Carol Rand raised her hand. "Sister, how did Bartlett get his name?"

"Remember Alan B. Shepard the first United States astronaut in space?" reminded Sister Magdalene. "Jimmy named his mouse after Shepard's middle name Bartlett."

"But Dixon can't send his mouse into space on Wednesday because we have school," blurted Dennis Drabek, attempting to undermine Jimmy's big day. "He will be missing class and get into trouble," he smirked.

"Almost true, Mr. Drabek," countered Sister Magdalene a

bit perturbed by his attitude. "But now I have a surprise for you all. Jimmy just asked me to invite the class to Bartlett's launch into space next week. I think it is a wonderful idea, so I will ask our principal Sister Mary Celeste if it could be arranged. With Sister's permission we will be able to go to the launch on Wednesday afternoon. It will be a perfect ending to our study of NASA's Project Mercury program. The launch site will be in a field about a ten-minute walk from the school grounds, so I will be sending permission slips home with you tomorrow for your parents to sign. Now before we continue our studies for the day, I would like to have Jimmy come up to the front of the class once again to read his essay."

"In conclusion, space flight will always be an important part of the future and will always stand out as a wonder that only a few can understand but that thousands can only imagine. If you are a man, woman, monkey or mouse you too can make your dream come true if you believe in it hard enough." Jimmy looked up from his essay, smiled and thanked the class while his fellow students clapped enthusiastically.

"Well done," said Sister Mary Magdalene as Jimmy returned to his desk.

"Now students, we will take a short break after which we will begin working on some geometry problems.

Please take out your math books and turn to page sixty-six." With that a collective groan went up from the class.

It was later that afternoon as Jimmy hurried to meet Elaine in the field where Bartlett was to be launched in seven days. As time was growing short, final details of the flight needed to be reviewed, so all would run smoothly. He could hardly contain himself as he sprinted across the field to tell her the good news.

"Elaine, Elaine! I won, I won! The book on the Mercury astronauts."

"Jimmy, that's wonderful," shouted Elaine. "I knew you could do it."

"Sister Mary Magdalene liked my essay so much she had me read it to the class. I've never had so many kids clap for me before."

"It sounds like you were the hero of the day."

"My parents were so pleased," Jimmy added, "they let me go to Rexall Pharmacy after school to buy something special."

"So, what did you get?" she inquired.

"Here," he handed Elaine a comic book, "your very own copy of *Strange Worlds*."

Elaine was overwhelmed. "Jimmy, you didn't have to do that."

"I know," he said sincerely, "but that's what friends do, they buy each other presents."

Elaine could only say "Thank you," through a veil of tears.

Chapter 22

Jimmy and Drabek

Jimmy awoke with a start. Something did not seem right. He quickly rolled over focusing through sleep-filled eyes upon the Mickey Mouse alarm clock sitting on his nightstand. Eleven o' clock! He could not believe he slept in so late. But Mickey was never wrong. It was Saturday and Elaine would be coming over in a few hours for a Bartlett training session. Jimmy dressed quickly, ran downstairs, and headed to the kitchen.

"Good morning, sleepy head," his mother Marge joked good-naturedly. "Hungry dear?"

"Not really Mom," Jimmy replied. "I need to run to Solon Hardware before Elaine arrives soon. I won't be long."

"Wow! Must be something very important," Marge inquired.

"I need to buy a new ball of kite string for next week's launch of Bartlett into space. I really do not trust the string I have now. Can't be too careful at this stage." With that Jimmy flew out the back door and into the garage. He jumped on his J.C. Higgins bicycle and pedaled as quickly as he could to Solon Hardware.

The day was sunny and clear with a refreshing chill in the air. But something bothered Jimmy. There was no wind! The leaves on the trees were completely calm. Normally he would not have given this a second thought. But with only four days left before launch Jimmy needed wind. Plenty of wind! There was no way at all he would be able to lift Bartlett in the air if the kite did not have generous gusts of wind pushing its sail. Certainly not with the extra weight of Bartlett in his cage attached to the cross bars of the kite. Successfully launching his furry astronaut into space was at the heart of his essay. But what if he failed? Would his classmates laugh at him? Was it a mistake to invite them in the first place? Even worse, what would Terri think of him? Then Jimmy thought of Vasco da Gama, Henry Hudson, Marco Polo and, of course, his favorite explorer Christopher Columbus. Had they not all taken risks? Was not the possibility of failure ever-present in their minds as they set out on their journeys? Jimmy knew the answer full well. Undaunted, he would move forward as they had, confident in the hours of preparation he and Elaine had put into this venture. But then he sighed, "I sure could use a windy day next Wednesday."

As Jimmy continued pedaling towards Solon Hardware, he suddenly had the distinct feeling he was being followed.

"Well, if it isn't Jimmy boy, Magdalene's new pet," boomed a voice from behind. Jimmy glanced back and to the right and was startled to see the rotund figure of Dennis Drabek quickly bearing down on him, his black Schwinn bicycle as menacing as its rider. Pulling even with Jimmy, the bully continued his taunts. "You think you're a big deal just because you won the essay contest. What did you do, clean Magdalene's erasers after school just to get in good with her?"

"You're a loser Dennis," Jimmy shot back. "Why don't you get lost!"

But Drabek was not finished. "Gee Jimmy boy, wouldn't it be tragic if something happened to your little rat before next week? Or, better yet, his cage comes loose from the kite and he falls to the ground like a dead bird in front of all your friends. Splaaat!"

As he continued his threats, Drabek's Schwinn increasingly drew closer to Jimmy's J. C. Higgins. "Move over, fatso!" Jimmy shouted. But the bully continued to close the gap between the two bikes. Suddenly, he gave a swift kick to Jimmy's back tire causing him to lose control. His front tire quickly veered to the left abruptly striking the curb. Jimmy was thrown head-first over the handlebars colliding violently with the sidewalk beyond.

"Hahahahahaha, have a good day," Drabek shouted

gleefully as he sped away.

Dazed, Jimmy lay on the ground for a few minutes. He was so stunned by what just happened that, at first, he did not feel the pain shooting from his right wrist. The throbbing became more intense as he reached down to lift his bicycle. Forgetting Drabek for the moment, all he could think of was next Wednesday and Bartlett's ride into space. If his wrist feels as badly then as it does now it will be impossible to maneuver the kite properly once Bartlett is in the air. Not to mention the preliminary details to be completed prior to liftoff. Drabek had won, he thought. With tears rolling down his cheeks, Jimmy slowly began walking his bike back home. The new ball of string was by now completely forgotten.

Chapter 23

Aftermath

Elaine shook her head in disbelief. "How can this have happened to Jimmy? It just isn't fair." It was late Saturday afternoon and she had just returned home from spending most of the day at the Dixon house with Jimmy. Hours before, she learned from Marge Dixon that Dennis Drabek caused him to have an accident on his bicycle and that he was with his father at the emergency room having his wrist x-rayed. When Jimmy returned home his right wrist was tightly wrapped and his arm in a sling.

"Oh Jimmy, I'm so sorry, are you okay?" Elaine asked sympathetically.

"Jimmy is very lucky he didn't hit his head on the sidewalk," said his father. "His wrist is sprained very bad, and he's bruised and scraped on his elbows and hands. But Jimmy is a fighter. He should be back hitting home runs this summer in a few weeks."

Jimmy could only smile weakly. His only concern was for

Bartlett and that next week's launch was over. His mother would call Sister Mary Magdalene about the unfortunate news.

"I'm okay, I guess, Elaine. Mr. and Mrs. Drabek are planning to meet with Mom and Dad after dinner to apologize for their son. They offered to pay any medical expenses. Dennis denies everything and refuses to admit any wrongdoing."

"Well, what do you expect?" said Elaine shaking her head. "He is simply a nasty person. They really have their hands full with that troublemaker."

"But it's only Saturday Jimmy," replied Elaine. "I'll work with Bartlett tomorrow while you rest. We still have Monday and Tuesday after school together to get him ready for his Wednesday launch."

Jimmy shook his head. "No, I don't think so, Elaine. There is no way I will be able to handle the kite on my own next week, especially if my wrist is hurting as badly as it does now. I know Sister Magdalene will understand. At least I won the essay contest. I think I'll go upstairs to my room for a while." As Jimmy began to walk away, he turned suddenly and looked at Elaine. "Thank you for all your help," he smiled.

"You're welcome, Jimmy. I had fun with you and Bartlett."

Elaine sat Indian style on her bed. She could not stop

thinking of Jimmy. Sure, he was disappointed that Bartlett would never fly in space, as was she. But whatever the case, for Elaine, Jimmy was an inspiration. She admired his sense of curiosity and adventure, how he loved to explore. Most of all, Elaine was fully on board with his newfound interest in the exploration of space. Her collaboration with Jimmy only fueled her fire and proved her conviction that men *and* women could successfully work together towards a common goal.

Mildred Shiver poked her head into Elaine's bedroom. "Dinner will be ready in five minutes," she announced.

"I'll be down soon, Mom."

"By the way, Elaine, I'm sorry that Jimmy had an accident. But thank goodness you will not have to be preoccupied with that mouse anymore. I thought it was silly from the beginning and nothing would come of it. It's time you started acting like a woman and not being concerned with such childish ideas."

As Mildred turned and walked away Elaine jumped from her bed and exclaimed in frustration, "I just lost my appetite, Mom!" Then she closed her door with authority, turning the key convincingly with a loud click, the sound reverberating through the upstairs hallway.

Chapter 24

To the Rescue

"Please be seated class," said Sister Mary Magdalene. "I have an important announcement to make." It was Monday morning and the bell had just rung for the start of the school day. Many of Jimmy's friends were gathered around him concerned with what had happened over the weekend.

"Are you okay, Jimmy?" wondered Lee.

"Was it an accident?" asked Doreen.

"Does it hurt?" inquired Janie.

Once the class had quieted, Sister Mary Magdalene began to speak. "This is the last week of school before summer vacation," she began. "Today and tomorrow, we will continue our final lessons of the year, on Thursday you will begin tidying up your desks and assist in cleaning the classroom, and on Friday Monsignor Mazer will be stopping by to give you your report cards. Finally, on Wednesday, as you are aware, Jimmy Dixon, the winner of the class essay contest had kindly invited us to the official launch into space of Bartlett his astronaut. However, due to Jimmy's unfortunate accident over the weekend the launch has been cancelled. Jimmy felt it would be impossible to successfully maneuver the kite alone with one arm in a sling. It would simply be too dangerous for Bartlett."

"Tough luck, Jimmy," said Joe.

"We understand," added Andrea sympathetically.

"You're the best, Jimmy," shouted Bill from the back of the room.

All the while Dennis Drabek sat glaring at Jimmy with smug satisfaction. "I guess you're not the winner of the essay contest after all," he said sarcastically. "You didn't complete the project!"

"Back off Drabek or I'll bop you in the face after school!" threatened Lee.

"That's enough from both of you," cautioned Sister Mary Magdalene. "One more outburst like that and the rest of your day will be spent in the principles' office with Sister Mary Celeste."

"Sorry, Sister," apologized Lee.

Dennis Drabek said nothing.

When the class settled down, Sister Mary Magdalene continued speaking. "I want to congratulate Jimmy a final time for his wonderfully written essay. He certainly deserved to win the book on the Mercury astronauts. I hope you enjoy it, Jimmy. Now students, please take out your math workbooks and we will begin to solve some story problems.

Suddenly, Terri raised her right hand.

"Yes, what is it, Terri?" said Sister Mary Magdalene.

"Before we begin our lesson, may I say something, please?" Sister Magdalene nodded her approval.

"Jimmy worked very hard writing his essay. He also spent a great deal of time preparing Bartlett for his trip into space. It would be a shame if he were not able to launch his kite on Wednesday after all that effort. With your permission, Sister Magdalene, I would like to assist Jimmy in completing the final phase of his project and fulfilling his goal. I just know I can do it."

"But how can you be so sure, Terri? It's only two days until Wednesday."

"Well, Sister Magdalene, Jimmy's next-door neighbor, Elaine Shiver, a freshman at the high school, has been assisting him with his project from the very beginning. She is a very nice person. I know Elaine can teach me. Please, give us a chance."

"What do you think, Jimmy?" said Sister Mary Magdalene looking his way.

Jimmy sat transfixed for a moment not believing that Terri would do this for him. Then suddenly he shouted, "Let's do it!" a big smile sweeping across his face.

"Yes, indeed, let's do it," exclaimed Sister Mary Magdalene pumping her fist in the air with enthusiasm.

The students began to chant. "Terri Rah, Terri Rah, Rah, Rah, Terri!"

Drabek was furious. "At least we'll get out of school for a few hours on Wednesday," he barked, in a weak attempt to justify the disappointment in his failed plan.

"Mr. Drabek, I have just about had it with you constantly speaking out of turn in my class," announced an angry Sister Magdalene. "You have now earned yourself a ticket to the principal's office after school."

At that, the class exploded with laughter.

Chapter 25

Countdown

Bartlett climbed off his exercise wheel, sipped water from his drip bottle, then burrowed into the wood shavings in the corner of his cage. At the same time, Jimmy crawled into bed. Tomorrow was the big day. He was nervous but felt he and Elaine had prepared well for Bartlett's ride into space. "Sleep tight my astronaut," he whispered.

But sleep did not come quickly for Jimmy. His thoughts turned to both Elaine and Terri. He admired Elaine for her determination and grit. Often during their training sessions with Bartlett, she would confess to him how ridiculous her mother behaved regarding their collaboration. "You're in high school," Mildred observed, "why must you hang around with a boy in grade school who is two years younger than you? People will begin talking." But Elaine was strong willed, and Jimmy liked that. "I wish she could be there to see the launch tomorrow," he sighed. However, he knew Elaine's mother would not allow her to skip school. As for Terri, well, what could he say? He respected her for many reasons. Yet, the way she stood up in class to rescue him was as heroic as the explorers and adventurers he revered. Jimmy had no problem at all working and sharing ideas with a girl. Soon, he drifted off to sleep.

As Jimmy struggled to fall asleep, Sister Mary Magdalene knelt in silent bedtime prayer.

Her small room at the convent housing the nuns of St. Rita Church was humble in its simplicity.

She had been a nun for well over thirty years, twelve of which was her present teaching assignment at the grade school. As Sister Magdalene prayed, her thoughts turned to Jimmy and all that he had been through. She envied his strength and ability to overcome adversity as well as his spirit of adventure. Most of all, she applauded his dedication to the Mercury astronauts and what they represented.

"Oh, to be young again," she thought out loud. Yet, she wondered. "Did I really choose the right path?" Such doubts plagued Sister Magdalene from time to time. She had entered the convent immediately after completing the eighth grade. Coming from an Irish family of seven children, her parents considered it a badge of honor for a daughter to become a nun or a son to join the priesthood as her older brother Tom had done.

"Did I rush into the religious life rather than first experiencing *this life* and all it has to offer?" As quickly as they entered her mind, such thoughts were brushed aside by Sister Magdalene. Of course, she had been dedicated to her calling from the very beginning. Her satisfaction was ultimately derived from doing God's work and carrying out his plan. High on that list was the commitment to her students, being a beacon of what was truly important in life, both spiritually and as a human creation of God here on Earth. Finally, she offered a silent prayer for the success of tomorrow's launch of Bartlett into space. Sister Mary Magdalene too was soon fast asleep.

It was close to noontime on launch day when Jimmy set out for the field from which Bartlett would be sent into space. The day was partly cloudy and overcast. Although a brisk breeze ruffled the treetops, he was still concerned whether the wind would be strong enough to properly elevate the kite. In his good hand Jimmy carried Bartlett's cage while in the other his fingers were clenched gingerly around the crossbar of the Strat-O-Flier despite the sling. Although his right wrist ached, more hurtful was Drabek's attempt to sabotage his project which he had worked so hard to complete. Yet, it made him more determined to succeed. When he arrived at the field, he gently set the cage down. Bartlett was on his exercise wheel early in the morning, but now he was sound asleep in his hidey hole. As Jimmy looked up, he could see Terri running across the field toward him. In her left arm she carried a brown paper bag.

"Hey, Tom Corbett," she waved cheerfully. Jimmy smiled broadly and waved back. Sister Mary Magdalene allowed he and Terri to miss the morning classes at St. Rita to prepare for the flight. After lunch Sister and their classmates would make the short ten-minute walk to the field from the school grounds.

"What's in the bag?" inquired Jimmy.

"Lunch," said Terri. "Peanut butter and jelly sandwiches and Hostess Twinkies for dessert. We can share the Coca Cola. I brought two paper cups."

They ate silently for a time, sitting cross-legged under the shade of a nearby tree. Then Jimmy spoke. "Listen, Terri," he said with sincerity. "Before our class arrives, I just want to thank you for all you have done. You have been my cheerleader since the day Sister Magdalene announced the essay contest. You're the best!"

Terri smiled at Jimmy. "So are you," she said softly. "Ready to launch *our* astronaut?"

"Ready as I'll ever be," Jimmy nodded confidently. "Let's do a final review before the class gets here," he suggested.

"Kite, check."

"Extra string, check."

"Capsule, check."

"Bartlett, check."

"Ground control, that's us," laughed Terri.

"Alright, that's everything," said Jimmy. "Now when we are ready to go, I will put Bartlett in the capsule while you unravel the string. Since I am taller, I will hold the kite up while you run with it. Once he is airborne, I will dash over to you in case you need any assistance. I know you'll do fine," he winked.

"Aye, aye, sir," saluted Terri.

Soon Sister Mary Magdalene and her seventh-grade class arrived at the field marching two-by-two, in an orderly manner, with girls in the front and boys in the back. The exception was Dennis Drabek positioned next to his teacher for obvious reasons.

"Good afternoon Jimmy and Terri, we are all so excited to be here," said Sister smiling. "Now students, please sit down on the grass and may I remind you that there will be no talking or fooling around unless you want to pay a visit to the principal's office later today. Do I make myself clear, Mr. Drabek?"

"*Oh yes*, Sister Mary Magdalene, I will be on my *very* best behavior," promised Dennis smirking ever so slightly.

"I'm sure you will, Dennis," responded Sister.

Sister Magdalene again turned to the class. "Before the launch begins let us say a prayer together for a successful flight and Bartlett's safe return to Jimmy. "Our Father who art in Heaven," she began as the students followed her lead.

"St. Francis of Assisi, patron saint of animals."

"Pray for us," answered the class in unison.

By now, a few dark clouds started to roll in, and the wind began to quicken. "Yes!" exclaimed Jimmy excitedly, "more wind, just as I hoped."

"Must have been the class prayer," Terri joked.

"Yeah, a miracle," chuckled Jimmy.

Kneeling, he opened Bartlett's cage and gently lifted the field mouse out with his one good hand. Before placing his astronaut into the kite's capsule, Jimmy drew him close whispering softly, "Good luck, pal, I'll have you up and down in no time." The plan was to send Bartlett three hundred feet in the air, the equal of a twenty-seven-story building. He would stay aloft for about five minutes before descending.

"Ready for liftoff," shouted Jimmy. With that he gripped the kite tightly with one hand, raised it off the ground and held it high in the air. About fifty feet away, Terri was positioned at the other end of the string firmly holding the wooden grip. The class began the countdown "10 9 8 7 6 5 4 3 2 1 0 . . . liftoff!" On cue both Jimmy and Terri began to run simultaneously coordinating each other's speed. As Jimmy felt the kite string become taut, he released the Strat-O-Flier while a generous gust of wind filled its sail. The kite shot into the air. Bartlett was on his way as Jimmy's classmates cheered!

Jimmy sprinted over to Terri who firmly held the

wooden grip. "I'll stay close to you just in case," he said. "Once Bartlett reaches the maximum height marked on the string, we can begin estimating five minutes in the air before bringing him back down." Terri felt confident controlling the kite. If the wind held at its present strength, Jimmy could see no reason why this venture would not see a successful ending. As the Strat-O-Flier began to ascend Jimmy directed Terri to pull in on the line at regular intervals until the kite gained the necessary altitude to find a good steady wind.

"So far, so good," smiled Terri.

"I hope Bartlett is enjoying his ride," said Jimmy.

Up and away soared the kite inching closer to the three-hundred-foot altitude. As Jimmy watched transfixed hardly believing that this was all happening at last, he failed to notice that the sky was darkening, and the wind had picked up its tempo. "Maximum height," he informed Terri. The Strat-O-Flier settled in for the next five minutes at its highest elevation. Suddenly Terri felt a considerable tug on the kite string as the winds aloft started to strengthen. The kite began to toss back and forth with greater rapidity. All Jimmy could think of was that day in March when the storm snapped the string of his Strat-O-Flier and was gone forever. He did not want to lose Bartlett.

"Let's bring him down quickly," shouted Jimmy.

With a sense of urgency, Terri began to draw in the string as quickly as possible intent on bringing Bartlett to safety. As the wind continued blowing stronger, she found it extremely difficult to control the kite. Sensing Terri's dilemma, Jimmy snatched the wooden grip away from her with his free hand. All at once, the kite began to nosedive. Attempting to bring it back under control with one hand, Jimmy was pulled by the wind and lost momentum, falling face first on to the ground, his right wrist throbbing. He could feel his fingers beginning to unravel from the wooden grip. Just as Jimmy was about to let go, a hand reached out to secure the kite. Jimmy looked up. It was Elaine. "Don't worry Jimmy, I've got this," she smiled. Her two feet firmly planted on the ground Elaine successfully brought Bartlett to safety.

Sister Mary Magdalene rushed to assist Jimmy. "I'm okay, I'm really okay," he looked up calling out to her. At that she stopped and offered a prayer of gratitude for Jimmy's welfare and Bartlett's safe return.

The class cheered wildly. Terri ran over to the kite to release Bartlett from his capsule. "He's fine," she shouted to Jimmy.

As relieved as he was to hear the good news, he still could not believe what Elaine had done. Jimmy lifted himself from the ground. "Aren't you supposed to be in school?" was all he could say.

"Well, Mom thinks so," she laughed. "I couldn't miss this for the world!"

Chapter 26

Letting Go

Ted Dixon poked his head into Jimmy's bedroom. "Play some catch, son?" he asked.

"Not now, Dad," Jimmy replied glumly.

"Are you OK?"

"Sure, Dad, I just don't feel like it."

It was late afternoon, the first Friday of Jimmy's summer vacation. Ordinarily he would have jumped at the opportunity of playing catch with his dad, especially with opening day of Little League season a week away. But Bartlett was on his mind. As for Elaine, she was so proud of Jimmy and his achievement and had nothing but good feelings about Terri and her contribution. She was thrilled that the launch was a huge success as dramatic as it may have been. As Sister Mary Magdalene was heard to say when she intervened to rescue Jimmy *and* Bartlett from impending disaster, "may the saints preserve us!"

Although her mother Mildred continued to cast a negative eye upon it all, Elaine's view of herself as a forward-looking woman continued to grow. But now that the adventure was over Jimmy had a big decision to make. Baseball could wait. He needed advice which only Elaine and Terri could provide. Jimmy felt that Bartlett could not live in his bedroom forever. He had been a brave little astronaut especially during his wild ride on the Strat-O-Flier last Wednesday. Both girls agreed with Jimmy that Bartlett deserved to go home.

Jimmy climbed into his bed that night. Then he climbed back out. He walked quietly over to Bartlett's cage, picked it up, then gently placed it on the bed next to his pillow. Bartlett was sound asleep snuggled deep in the comfort of his wood shavings. "I'm sure going to miss you Bartlett," Jimmy said. "You are the best pal ever. But you need to go back home to your mom and dad. I hope they were not too worried about you. They will be so glad to see you." With that, Bartlett's tiny ears perked-up. Shaking wood shavings from his fur, he made his way towards Jimmy's face peering through the bars of the cage. Sniffing the air twice, he recognized Jimmy's familiar scent. Then he curled up close to the side of the cage and went back to sleep.

Early Saturday morning Jimmy crossed Linden Drive heading for the woods which rimmed the far end of the cornfield behind Eagleton's house. Bartlett was safely nestled in both his hands. Suddenly, he stopped and looking back saw Elaine and Terri calling out to him and waving. "What are you two doing here?" a surprised Jimmy wondered.

"Doll told me last night what you planned for Bartlett this morning," explained Elaine, "so, I called Terri and here we are."

"We wanted to give you some moral support," added Terri.

"You guys are the best," laughed Jimmy.

As the trio drew closer to the edge of the woods Jimmy suddenly stopped and fell silent, tears rolling down his cheeks. Terri hugged him gently. "Oh, Jimmy," she said, "I know this is a sad moment for you, but it is the right thing to do. Bartlett is going home."

Jimmy sighed. "Well, it's time," he said, "let's go." As he began to walk into the woods, he noticed both Elaine and Terri did not follow.

"We thought you should be alone with Bartlett at the end," they explained. Jimmy smiled gratefully.

Soon he came to the spot where he and Elaine first found Bartlett so many weeks ago. Jimmy paused for a moment. A slight breeze, the breath of God, arose to comfort him. He gently drew Bartlett to his cheek feeling his soft fur against his skin for the last time. Finally, Jimmy knelt on one knee, carefully placed his astronaut on the ground then watched as he slowly disappeared into the silence and serenity of the woods. Goodbye, Bartlett," he said quietly. "You will always be my hero."

Chapter 27

Resolution

Mildred slowly lifted her head and glanced at the clock sitting on the nightstand beside her bed. Through weary eyes she read: 3:00 am. "Always 3:00 am," she whispered to herself, "just as last night and the night before that and the night before that." Mildred had not slept soundly in over two weeks.

Husband Ed snored loudly next to her. Yet the noise could not drown out the sound playing inside her head. Slowly like a dripping faucet, "click, click, click," repeatedly over, and over again. Louder and louder.

Mildred was frightened. "I'm losing her, I'm losing Elaine." Ever since she told her daughter it was time to act like a woman now that Jimmy and his childish mouse adventure was over, they hardly spoke to one another. "Elaine has shut me out of her life!" The sound of the lock turning in Elaine's bedroom door that day haunted her. "Click, click, click."

Suddenly, Mildred began to shake Ed vigorously.

Startled, her husband nearly fell out of bed. "Mildred, Mildred," he shouted, "what on Earth is going on? Are you okay?"

Mildred began to cry. "Ed, where have I gone wrong with Elaine? She never speaks to me anymore. She avoids me every chance she has. I have tried to be a good mother, giving her the same advice my own mother gave me. It's just not working."

Ed yawned momentarily. "Well, of course, it's not working," he responded. "Your mother was from a different generation than Elaine, as you are. Sure, we want the best for Elaine; to marry a fine man someday and to be a good mother. I have seen her frustration with you but have not offered my opinion in the hope that the two of you would work things out together. Why don't you just give Elaine a chance and see her point of view for a change? It does not mean you cannot give her guidance as you see fit. To tell you the truth, I have been silently rooting for Elaine and her wish to explore new paths in her life." Ed chuckled. "Who knows, she may be the first female president of the United States someday. Now march down the hall and tell your daughter that you love and support her."

"But Ed, it's after 3:00 am! What if she locks the door on me again?"

"Enough, Mildred, just go!"

Mildred quietly turned the doorknob of Elaine's room and walked in silently. Hesitant at first, she finally sat down on the edge of the bed then gently touched her daughter's shoulder. "Elaine, Elaine," she softly called. "It's me, Mom, wake up, dear."

At first Elaine thought she was dreaming until the face of her mother slowly came into focus in the twilight of her room. "Mom, what's wrong, what's the matter?"

Mildred's voice quivered. "Oh, Elaine," she replied, "I love you very much and am so proud you are my daughter. Please, forgive me for not believing in you."

As if a weight had been lifted from Elaine's shoulders, she threw her arms around Mildred and hugged her affectionately for what seemed like an eternity. "I love you too, Mom. Thanks for being my mother." With tearful eyes, Mildred gave Elaine a final kiss then gently tucked her under the covers. For the remainder of the night both mother and daughter slept soundly, each dreaming beautiful dreams and smiling peacefully.

The End

www.ingramcontent.com/pod-product-compliance
Lightning Source LLC
LaVergne TN
LVHW011841060526
838200LV00054B/4122